To Make a Wee Moon

To Make a Wee Moon

PHYLLIS REYNOLDS NAYLOR

Illustrations by Beth and Joe Krush

FOLLETT PUBLISHING COMPANY Chicago New York

SBN 695-40058-4 Titan edition
SBN 695-80058-2 Trade edition

Library of Congress Catalog Card Number: 79-83313

First Printing   I

To John and Nancy

IF GRANDMOTHER were going to eat anybody, Jean decided, it would have to be Brian. She certainly wasn't going to let the old woman eat her. In fact, she was determined not to let anything at all upset her, for it would all be over in a matter of months, and there had been trouble enough as it was.

"Oh, Angus, she'll eat them alive!" Mother had said grimly that morning as they placed the old brown suitcase in the car. "Grandmother and her superstitions! They'll be terrified."

But Father's voice was steady. " 'Twill do her good to have young ones in the house again. And Gwen's there. They'll manage."

Now the train was stopping again. Jean McGinnis's dark blond head jerked forward, her chin scraping the buttons on her plaid coat.

"Is it Oshkosh?" asked Brian, rising up on the seat beside her. "Are we there yet?"

"No," Jean answered. "Go back to sleep."

She tried to remember what the old lady looked like, but couldn't. All that came to mind when she thought of Grandmother was the wind, a gigantic hurricane, perhaps, with Grandmother in the center. The wind, the stars, night, and a few notes of a song which Jean remembered from long ago.

Jean leaned back and studied her face in the window glass. Two dark brown eyes stared back, like another young girl looking in. Her face was as round as a dinner plate, with two small delicate ears on each side. "The handles on a sugar bowl," Mother always said. Her cheeks were unusually red. They had always been that way, and so had Brian's. But her lips were much too thin. No lips and scarcely any eyebrows. "That's okay, lass," Father always said. "The eyes and the cheeks make up for it."

Her fingers still felt sticky from the peanut butter sandwiches. Jean reached in the big paper sack for the washcloth, and carefully wiped each finger, wondering what Grandmother would say when she saw how dirty and wrinkled she and Brian looked after the long ride. She imagined the old woman snatching the washcloth and rubbing their faces raw.

There was an old lady from Oshkosh, who smothered us both with a washcloth. The nonsense words were getting sillier, and Jean laughed to herself. Brian sat up.

"What are you laughing at?"

Jean leaned over. "There was an old lady from Oshkosh, who smothered us both with a washcloth," she whispered.

Brian giggled. "There was an old lady from Oshkosh, who smothered us both with a washcloth," he repeated. "There was an old lady. . . ."

"Shhhh," said Jean, as the people across the aisle looked around.

". . . from Oshkosh, who smothered us both with a washcloth," Brian continued. "There was an old. . ."

Jean reached for the paper sack on the floor and dug down inside it. "Here," she said, thrusting something in his hands.

It was an old, black, squat, hunk of a pipe that Father had given Brian when he was five. "Here, lad, a 'membrance of your Grandfather McGinnis," he had said, playfully thumping Brian on the head with it. If he had known then how Brian would carry it around in his pocket, how he would take it to kindergarten, and hide it under his pillow at night, he might not have done so.

Now, with the end of the thing in his mouth, the big bowl hanging down on his chin and chest, Brian grew quiet and leaned back in the seat beside Jean.

"Don't get the pipe out unless you have to," Mother had warned as she put Jean and Brian on the train and handed them the sack of "necessaries."

"I had to," Jean said to herself as the train went clicking on down the track.

There was an old lady from Oshkosh, who smothered us both with a washcloth.

Something about night made her lonely. During the day, Jean hadn't thought about her parents at all. It had been easy getting on the train that afternoon and waving at them through the window. But now, the bustle and noise were gone, and the other passengers had curled up on their seats to sleep. The quiet of night made her homesick.

"McGinnis, eh?" The conductor stopped to chat. "Going to Oshkosh, huh?"

"Yes."

"Well, we won't be there till tomorrow noon, so might as well get some sleep."

Brian was sleeping soundly, the pipe still resting on his chest. The conductor lifted him up and placed him on the seat behind Jean. Then he went swaying down the aisle in rhythm with the moving car.

Jean drew her legs up and covered them with the hem of her coat. She wasn't the least sleepy. The rapid click of the train as it sped over the rails seemed a roar in her ears, and a draft from the open door made goose flesh on her bare legs.

She did not seem to fit on the seat. She turned over and faced the other way, but then her back grew cold.

If she weren't so cold, she wouldn't be homesick, Jean decided. She thought about her bed at home, the narrow cot in the living room behind the coal stove. There it was warm, and she could fall asleep to the clink of cinders. A wave of panic raced through her again. It wasn't home anymore, because Father was selling the house. Home, for now, was Oshkosh, with Grandmother McGinnis and Aunt Gwen, and Jean couldn't even remember what they looked like.

The train screeched to a stop, started again, and the *clicka clicka* grew faster. Jean's head rocked back and forth and the noise made her drowsy. Slowly her hands and feet began to feel heavy, and the clanks and rustlings from outside the coach became a part of her dreams.

Jean opened her eyes. She had been sleeping, she knew, because she'd dreamed it was time to get off and she couldn't find Brian. She sat up and looked over the seat. Brian was fast asleep, his mouth half open, little bubbly sounds coming from his lips.

Jean leaned back and looked out the window. She could see a clock on the side of a depot. Two o'clock in the morning. The car was filled with the assorted snores and grunts of the other sleepers, and Jean smiled to herself. It sounded as though they were singing a chorus.

She did not sleep any more. At four o'clock she was still awake. Gradually the people around her began to stir. Jean got up and straightened her coat, feeling less alone now that everyone else was waking. Brian, however, slept on, so Jean went to the bathroom to wash.

She was just coming back when she heard Brian sobbing loudly.

"There's your sister, buddy," a man was saying to the chubby boy who sat half-yawning, half-crying, in his rumpled coat. "I told you she wouldn't go off and leave you."

Jean sat down and combed his hair. "Let's go have breakfast," she said brightly. "We get to eat in the dining car this time."

A white-jacketed waiter led them to a table with a rose in a vase and pulled out Jean's chair for her.

Jean awkwardly opened the menu and scanned the prices quickly. Orange juice, forty cents. She looked quickly at the waiter and back again. It couldn't be right! Eggs and toast and bacon, two dollars!

"Milk," Jean ordered. "Milk and cinnamon buns."

"I want Wheaties," Brian said loudly.

The waiter looked at Jean.

"No," Jean told him. "Just milk and buns."

Brian started to protest, but just then a short man and a woman with a great fur piece around her shoulders stopped at the table.

"If you care to wait, sir, we'll have another table in a moment," the headwaiter said, but the grand lady sat down beside Brian.

"This is fine," the short man said, "if the little lady doesn't mind sharing the table." He pulled out the chair beside Jean.

Jean flushed and unfolded the napkin on her lap.

"And what's your name, little fellow?" the man said to Brian.

There was no answer.

"Ah!" said the woman. "Cat's got his tongue, I'll bet."

Still no answer. Jean slowly raised her eyes. There sat Brian with Grandfather McGinnis's old pipe in his mouth, and he had filled the bowl of the pipe with ice from his water glass. Instead of answering, he was breathing through the pipe, and water came spluttering out the other end.

"Brian!" Jean said. "The man asked you a question."

In answer, Brian waggled his head back and forth so that the pipe swayed.

"It's all right," said the man, smiling. "I hope you won't mind if we join you. We get off at Chicago and would like to have breakfast before we go."

The waiter took their orders and left, and the woman turned to Jean. "Where are you from, dear, and where are you going?"

"From Logan, West Virginia," Jean said. "We're going to Oshkosh to live with my grandmother until Daddy and Mother come for us. They have to sell the house first."

"I see." The woman folded her hands. One skinny finger had three rings on it, and Jean could not help staring. "Well, it must be quite exciting taking a train trip alone. What does your father do?"

"He was a coal miner," Jean answered, running one finger over the spoon at her plate. "When he comes to Oshkosh, he'll work on a dairy farm."

"That will be nice," the man said.

Jean suddenly felt very hot. The dining car was overheated. She longed to take off her coat, but remembered the big mended place under one sleeve of her dress.

The waiter arrived with both orders and quickly placed them on the table. First came a platter of eggs and sausage for the man, griddle cakes and syrup for the lady and then the milk and buns for Jean and Brian.

Jean knew exactly what was going to happen, but she could not stop it. Brian took one look at the lady's plate and then his own and said, "I don't want this old bun, Jean. I want what she's got."

Jean's face turned crimson. This time she could not even speak. She glared across the table, and Brian sunk down in his chair.

"Well, why can't I have what she's having?" he asked timidly.

"We're having milk and buns," Jean said tersely. "Eat your breakfast, Brian, and hush."

"If the boy wants some griddle cakes, I'll be glad

14

to order some for him," the man said.

"No, thank you," said Jean. "We have plenty."

She hated the train then. She hated the old suitcase tucked under the seat, the crumpled lunch sack, and the dress beneath the plaid coat.

"Chicago!" called the conductor from the doorway. "Chicago in five minutes."

The woman in the fur piece dabbed at her mouth with her napkin and looked at Jean over the tops of her jeweled glasses. "I can't possibly finish my plate," she said. "If you don't mind, I'd be glad to let your brother have the two cakes that are left."

Jean did not answer. For a brief moment she thought that the jeweled glasses were magic, that the woman in the fur could see right through Jean's coat. She could see the mend under the sleeve and on inside, where Jean's heart was sooty with the coal dust of Logan, West Virginia.

As the couple said good-bye and left, Brian slowly reached over and pulled the lady's plate toward him. With one eye on Jean, he carefully ate the remaining griddle cakes, savoring the syrup, and rubbed his finger over the plate when he was through.

Jean did not scold him. She sat with her eyes in her lap and, when he was finished, led him back to the coach car. All she wanted was enough clothes, enough food, and enough money so as not to feel different.

Chapter 2

EARLY THAT AFTERNOON, the train stopped for the last time. The conductor hustled the bags out the door, gave his arm to Jean, and lifted Brian to the ground.

"Hope you like Oshkosh," he smiled. "Wrong time of year to be comin', though."

The moment Jean stepped out on the ground in three inches of snow, the cold wind cut through her coat, tossing her hair wildly about her head and shoulders. She covered her nose and mouth with her coat collar and looked around for her grandmother and aunt.

Suddenly a pair of warm arms engulfed both Jean and Brian at once, and a head of thick blond hair nuzzled their faces. When the big arms stopped squeezing, the blond head rose up, up, and when it finally stopped, Jean was dismayed to find that Aunt

Gwen was a veritable giant of a lady, even taller than Father. As Jean stared up at the woman, whose eyes were as sparkly as two great stars, she fancied that Aunt Gwen looked like Glinda, the Good Witch of the South in the *Wizard of Oz*.

"Jean and Brian!" cried Aunt Gwen, her warm breath making a cloud of mist about her face. "I'm so glad you're here!" And again the blond head swooped down and the long arms engulfed them.

" 'Tis a bitter day an' they've no boots on their feet!" exclaimed a voice behind them.

Jean turned to see a squat woman in a gray coat hobbling toward her. The old grandmother seemed almost as wide as Aunt Gwen was tall. Scowling and smiling in a unique expression of welcome, she reached out and folded one of Jean's hands in hers.

"Icicles!" she exclaimed. "Ha'e ye no mittens wi' ye?" And then, without waiting for an answer, she herded them toward the car while Aunt Gwen followed behind with the suitcase.

The car was old and smelled of walnuts. From one corner of the back seat, Jean watched Aunt Gwen with curious fascination. Even sitting down, Aunt Gwen's head almost touched the roof of the car, and her big hands looked like a man's as they guided the steering wheel. Her features were large, even her ears, and the way she shoved her hair behind them made them look bigger still. Her nose was pinched in the middle, a little too narrow for her face, and her skin was covered from forehead to chin with small brown freckles which gave her the appearance of a huge, speckled egg. Her laugh was big too, and when she threw back her head, she made rich, chuckling noises in her throat.

But Grandmother wanted attention. "Like a balloon on a stick!" she exclaimed, peering at Jean over her glasses. "A big, round pumpkin o' a face, an' little stick arms an' legs. Jean, girl, wha' does your mither feed ye?"

Aunt Gwen laughed warmly. "But look at her cheeks! Did you ever see such beautiful red cheeks?"

"Humph," said Grandmother McGinnis, her scowl returning. "Makes her look healthier than she be."

Grandmother, in turn, was like a balloon all over, short and squat and fat, with large jowls hanging all the way down her neck, and thick legs that swelled out over the tops of her tight black galoshes. Her hair was very thin, pulled back tight from her face, and her eyes were small and intense. Just like a rooster's, Jean decided.

"Well, tell us now," said Aunt Gwen. "How was the trip?"

"It was too long," said Brian. "Next time I wanna come on an airplane."

"There'll be no next time, honey," Aunt Gwen said. "You're here to stay. Oh, you're going to love the farm! Wait till spring!"

But spring was a long time away from the middle of February, and as the car groaned its way out of the city, past the frozen fields, the homesickness welled up in Jean again. She wished she could just skip the next few months until her parents came.

It was late afternoon before the car pulled up the long drive to the small stucco house in the walnut trees, far out in the frozen countryside around Osh-kosh. Beyond the trees stood the old barn, the silo, a corn crib, and tractor shed. And then, beyond that, as far as the eye could see, was nothing but the white of the fields, broken only by an occasional clump of trees or the dull red roof of a farmhouse.

"It's spooky here," Brian said, as the wind made a rushing noise in the dead branches of the trees over-head.

"Don't talk so," Grandmother grunted, her eyes drifting to the trees. "The Little Folk won't hear i' ye don't call them."

Little folk? Jean wondered. But before she could ask any questions, Aunt Gwen rushed them on into the house.

"Don't trouble yourselves about the fairies," Gwen said. "There's enough to happen without elves, too."

They entered the back porch, filled with the warm smell of fresh milk, past the pump and dipper, and into the big kitchen with its great white table in the center, already set with blue and white china for four.

They got no further. Aunt Gwen took their coats, Grandmother set them at the table, and the next Jean knew, the kettle was singing on the stove. Grandmother placed huge bowls of oatmeal on their plates with little pitchers of cream on the side. When Brian hesitated, Grandmother picked up a spoonful of porridge and dipped it in the cream, then handed it to Brian who swallowed it dutifully.

Big puffy muffins came next, dripping with butter; boiled eggs, sliced and creamed; and bananas with sugar. It was breakfast, lunch, and supper combined, for by the time they had finished eating and answering questions, it was almost five o'clock. Grandmother McGinnis hobbled about between table and stove, her eyes on the trees outside the window, and her ears to the wind in the chimney. When the afternoon shadows mingled with the darkness that settled down over the frozen ground, she clicked her teeth and talked about bedtime.

"Oh, let's let them stay up a bit," Aunt Gwen said, and began singing a song in a high, thin voice:

Auld Daddie Darkness
Creeps fra' his hole,
Black as a blackamoor,
Blind as a mole.
Stir the fire till it glows,
Let the bairnie sit,
Auld Daddie Darkness
Is not wanted yit.

" 'Tis been a long time since I've heard tha' song," said Grandmother.

"It's been a long time since this house had children," said Gwen.

Jean was helping Grandmother stack the blue and white china by the sink when the loud ringing of the telephone on the wall startled her. A blue and white plate slipped from her hand and clattered into the sink, cracking down the middle.

Jean looked quickly at Grandmother, the blood rising to her face. "Oh, I'm sorry!" she said miserably.

Grandmother started to answer, but Aunt Gwen was holding the phone toward Jean. "It's your mother," she smiled.

Jean rushed to the phone as though she were rushing to her mother's arms.

Mother's voice sounded tinny, and far away. "Is everything all right, dear? Did the trip go okay?"

"Yes. Everything's fine," Jean said, conscious of Grandmother watching. "I guess I'm a little homesick."

"Oh, darling, I know you are, but it won't be long before your father and I get there. I just wanted to be sure you made it all right and that Brian didn't get sick."

"No, he's all right," Jean said. "We didn't have any trouble on the train. Not really."

"Well, I'm glad. We do miss you already. We're going to try hard to get there by spring."

Jean gave Brian the phone and listened glumly as he talked to Mother. "Yes . . . Yes . . . Okay . . . Huh uh . . . Okay . . . Good-bye."

"I'm sorry about the plate," Jean said, turning back to Grandmother.

"Might not ha'e been ye at a', Jean girl," her grandmother answered, a note of mystery in her voice.

Jean glanced quickly at Aunt Gwen. Of course it was she who dropped it! What could Grandmother mean?

Aunt Gwen rolled her eyes, smiling broadly. "That's right, Jean," she said. "Maybe the fairies just whisked the plate from your hands and crashed it down in the sink. Maybe you didn't have a thing to say about it."

Jean's eyes met Aunt Gwen's, and suddenly they were laughing silently together, enjoying the fun without another word spoken.

When Jean and Brian were dressed for bed, they sat down on the big plump sofa before the great fireplace, and Grandmother covered them with a quilt. A bowl of apples sat on the hearth with a bucket of chestnuts beside it, and Patches, the cat, slept between the two, her nose resting on two white paws.

Aunt Gwen sat down beside Brian, and Grandmother lowered herself into the old rocker. For a long time they sat without talking, watching the logs spit and crackle in the orange flames.

By and by Grandmother said to nobody in particular, " 'Tis a shameful waste o' pennies, I say, to be callin' across the country aboot the bairnies. Does she think we wouldn't call i' the children were not safe in oor house?"

"She only wanted to give them her love," Aunt Gwen said. "You can imagine how lonesome it is without them."

Grandmother grunted and clicked her teeth. "Many an evenin' yit to do withoot 'em. Might as well git used to it noo. Can't be callin' every night."

Jean listened silently. Was this the same granny that had rocked her to sleep as a baby, a dim blur in the far reaches of her memory? Was this what Mother meant about Grandmother eating people alive, sort of taking bites at them every now and then?

"It's been a long time since you were in this house," Aunt Gwen said, hugging Brian.

"I can't never remember it at all," Brian said.

"I know. You were much too small. But your family used to live here with us, and Grandmother and I used to take turns rocking you at night when the teething began."

Grandmother smiled as she watched the fire. "It was a good summer. Jean was barely four, an' a' over the farm, she was. We could hear her laughin' on the grass, an' the baby croonin' on the sun porch. 'Twas the last good summer."

"And then we moved to Logan?" Jean asked, not remembering.

Aunt Gwen didn't answer for a moment. "Yes,"

she said finally. "Then a friend wrote your father about a mining job, and Angus moved your whole family to West Virginia." She was not smiling now, and Grandmother's teeth began their rhythmical clicking.

"And I haven't seen you all these years since, have I?" asked Jean. "We didn't even get back to visit."

"Just your faither," said Grandmother. "For his Dad's funeral, tha' was a'." She stopped rocking and sat motionless. "Tha' was a'."

No one spoke for a while. Finally Aunt Gwen reached over and squeezed Jean's hand. "Anyway, you're back now, and we're glad to have you," she smiled.

Jean's eyes grew heavier and heavier as she watched the shadows flicker on the walls and listened to the creak of the rocker. Grandmother McGinnis sat with her hands folded in her great lap, and in the half darkness of the warm parlor, Jean fancied she saw the elves and fairies dancing about which had come with her from Scotland those many years ago.

There was an old lady from Oshkosh. . . . Jean stopped, almost afraid that Grandmother McGinnis could read her thoughts. But the old woman kept on rocking, her eyes on the fire and her ears to the wind.

Chapter 3

JEAN AWOKE the next morning long before her eyes opened. Back in Logan, she would have heard the clink of coals in the big black stove, and either her cheeks or her back would be toasty warm, depending on which side was facing the fire.

But now, bedded beneath a half dozen quilts, Jean could tell that the upstairs of the farmhouse was unheated, for her nose felt like an ice cube, and a cold draft chilled her forehead and ears. Finally, when she opened her eyes, the sun shining through the window almost blinded her, and the lacy pattern of ice on the window had begun to trickle and run in rivulets down the sill.

There were two bedrooms upstairs and one down. Grandmother and Brian slept in the one below, and the second upstairs bedroom was being saved for Father and Mother when they came. Jean turned over to peer at the bed beside hers, but it was already neatly made up.

Just then Aunt Gwen came into the room, wrapped in a huge flannel bathrobe. Her light blond hair was piled loosely on top of her head, long strands drifting down here and there, and she was smiling as brightly as the sun itself.

"It's church this morning, Jean," she said, flinging open the closet door and looking at Jean's dresses. "And where's your Sunday's?"

Jean sat up. Sunday's dress was also Tuesday's and Thursday's, and the other dress had to make do on Monday, Wednesday, and Friday. On Saturdays she was allowed to wear slacks.

"I don't have a Sunday dress," she said, dropping her legs over the side of the bed. "The blue one's better than the yellow, but it's got a mend on one side."

Aunt Gwen reached into the closet and pulled out a green dress that had been shoved back in one corner. "What about this?"

"Oh, it's so ugly!" Jean cried. "Please don't make me wear it to church!"

"Hmmmmm." Aunt Gwen held the plain, round-necked dress up. The sleeves flopped long and loose.

"Mother bought it on sale," Jean said miserably, "and I hate it. I just hate it."

Aunt Gwen twirled it around. "You know, Jean, it wouldn't take much at all to fix it up."

26

Jean got out of bed and wrapped one of the quilts around her. "How? It looks like a uniform for a girl's school."

Aunt Gwen laughed. "Why, Jean, we can make anything at all if we work at it hard enough. To make a wee moon, all we need is a little patience and a lot of hard work. A dress shouldn't be half that difficult. When you've eaten breakfast, come see what I've done with it."

There was no real bathroom in the house. There was a sink in the kitchen, a pump on the back porch, and a toilet and cold shower in the basement. Hot water came from big kettles which Grandmother heated on the stove. But this morning Grandmother ordered a shower and handed Jean a towel.

Jean went across the back porch and started down the basement steps at the rear. The cellar had a dank, earthy, apple smell, and Jean pulled her hand quickly away from the wall as it touched a cobweb. A mountain of corncobs rested beneath the steps, waiting to be fed into the great black stove in the kitchen, and the mysterious generator in one corner clanked and hummed as it went about its business of making electricity for the old farmhouse. In a small, adjoining room, jars of tomatoes, preserves, and string beans waited their turn on the table, and dusty bushels of onions and potatoes and apples lined the walls on either side.

Jean groped her way to the flowered curtain behind

the furnace. With a deep breath, she pulled off her gown and turned on the shower. The water was as cold as snow, and she leaped back out, while the pipe above rattled and shook and ordered her in once more.

Brian was already at the table, eating the heaping bowl of oatmeal before him, when Jean came back in the kitchen.

"It must be terribly cold out," Jean said, sitting down at her place.

"Aye, the coldest yit," Grandmother said, bustling over with a pan of rolls. Jean noticed that she wore a brown velvet dress with a brooch at the collar, and a smudge of flour on her cheeks and nose.

It was a huge breakfast of grilled kipper, rolls and marmalade, eggs, milk, and oatmeal. Jean could tell by the way Grandmother fussed over them that it wasn't every morning there were kippers for breakfast.

" 'Tis to fatten ye up before the spring grippe sets in," Grandmother said. "Try a little marmalade wi' your roll, Jean girl."

When breakfast was over, Jean went to the sun porch on the west side of the house where Aunt Gwen was working. There hung the dress, neatly pressed, and Jean could scarcely believe it was the same one. Over the high round neck, Aunt Gwen had tacked a white lacy collar. The sleeves which had been long and wide were now gathered at the edges with more white velvet ribbon, and the hem had been raised several inches to keep it in style.

28

"Oh, Aunt Gwen!" Jean walked around it, wide-eyed. "It's beautiful! Why, it's my best dress!" She turned suddenly and threw her arms around her aunt. She loved her then—the big ears and the big chin and the speckled-egg skin. She even loved the big hands, and the feet that took a size ten slipper at least. The bright sun seemed to warm her through as she put on the pretty dress and went to parade before Grandmother.

The small Presbyterian church on the hill had a long, winding driveway, and the big black car chugged and whined as it skidded its way to the top. Aunt Gwen took Grandmother's arm and helped her across the slippery flagstone walk.

Inside, the organ was already playing, as crisp and sharp as the icicles that hung along the roof. Grandmother McGinnis chose a pew halfway down, and guided Brian in ahead of her. Jean sat next to Grandmother, and Aunt Gwen came last. Gradually the music got louder and slower until suddenly the door on one side of the pulpit opened, and out came the minister and the choir. In their white robes, the singers looked like snowmen as they took their places in the choir loft, tall and straight and starched. The congregation rose as the minister led the call to worship, then sat down again. As the creaking of pews faded away, Jean realized that someone else was in the pew on the other side of Aunt Gwen.

Jean glanced quickly at the stranger. He was tall, perhaps the tallest man in the church. His face was so long that his eyes seemed unnaturally far from his mouth, and his light bushy eyebrows came together in the middle as though his whole face had been pushed in at the sides. The sleeves on his suit coat were too short, and he sat with one big unpolished shoe on the side of the other, his knees digging into the back of the pew in front.

Aunt Gwen continued to look straight ahead with a warm half-smile on her face as though the whole choir were singing just for her.

Later, when the congregation rose again for a hymn, Jean saw the stranger's hand fold over Aunt Gwen's on the bottom of the hymn book.

She stared up at her aunt and then down at the floor. It seemed like something she wasn't supposed to see. But when the music stopped and they all sat down, Aunt Gwen closed the book, and the man's two big hands rested on his knees again.

The sermon began, about the history of the Presbyterian church in Scotland. Each sentence started out low. Then the minister's voice grew higher and higher until it almost reached the end, where it dropped to its lowest point yet. On it went, the slow rising and falling while Jean tried to adjust to the hard pew beneath her.

Suddenly she heard a sharp tapping sound and

looked across Grandmother's wide lap to see Brian hitting the edge of his seat with a bamboo fan.

Slowly Grandmother McGinnis's hand left her lap. It went straight to Brian, took hold of the fan, and stuck it behind the hymnals.

The little boy scooted back in the pew restlessly, and began swinging his legs back and forth. Suddenly his extended feet hit the back of the front pew with a loud thump, and two ladies turned their heads, their lips pursed in annoyance. Again Grandmother's hand reached out, caught his legs, and thrust them down where they belonged.

The minister droned on and on. Jean wished that the history of the church in Scotland were not so long or so illustrious. Just when she was sure the minister was finishing, he would start on something new.

Grandmother began to doze. Her head began to nod and tip sideways, lower and lower. Slowly her mouth fell open, and a soft *zapping* sound came from her lips.

Brian's hand moved forward. Stealthily it clutched the pile of offertory envelopes on the back of the front pew. Slowly it brought the pile to his lap, where he methodically began licking each one and glueing it together.

"Brian!" Jean whispered, leaning forward.

He turned his head, grinned, and went on licking.

"Brian!" Jean whispered again. The ladies in front

pursed their lips. Jean tried to reach across Grandmother's lap, but Brian chuckled out loud and scooted away.

Suddenly Grandmother's head snapped forward, her mouth closed, and her small beady eyes opened wide. Like a streak of summer lightning, her hand shot out and grabbed all the envelopes. With a jerk it stuffed them back in the box on the pew. And then, Grandmother McGinnis opened her purse.

"Gum," thought Jean. But Brian was not to be rewarded. Instead, Grandmother brought out a rubber band. Deftly she slipped it on Brian's wrist. Then, while Brian stared, she caught the rubber band with one finger, pulled it back, and snapped it hard against his hand.

Instantly Brian pulled his hand away and stared at Grandmother. The old woman did not stare back. She closed her purse, folded her hands once more, and lifted her head toward the choir which was rising for the final hymn.

On the way home, Jean tried to think of a way to ask Aunt Gwen about the man who sat beside her in church. But the fact that he left as soon as the service was over made her hesitate.

Grandmother McGinnis, however, did not keep it secret.

"Donald Harvie was late for church this mornin', Gwendolyn," she said disapprovingly as they rounded the bend near the farmhouse. "Never did think much o' a man tha' couldn't get to service on time."

"The roads are bad today, Mother," Aunt Gwen said. "A lot of other people were late too."

"Donald Harvie would ha'e been late i' his car had wings," Grandmother said.

"Not necessarily," Aunt Gwen replied.

There was soup for dinner, or broth, as Grandmother called it, full of turnips and carrots and lamb. When the blue and white china had been washed and put away, Jean asked if she and Brian might explore the barn.

"Why, ye ha'e no boots and no mittens, girlie," said Grandmother.

But Aunt Gwen hustled up some of her own. "Don't pick up your feet," she laughed. "You'll leave the boots behind if you do." She buckled them around Jean's shoes and added, "There's a young girl up the road whose mother says she has a box of clothes for you, with a pair of boots, too. Tomorrow we'll go see what will do."

So Jean and Brian, clad in jackets much too big for them, floppy boots, and scarves wrapped around their mouths and noses, set out for the barn, shuffling along the narrow snowbanked path. Patches, the cat, followed hesitantly behind, gingerly testing each paw in the snow before putting it down.

They reached the shadow of the big gray barn, and Jean's fingers closed over the latch. *Creeeeak!* The door gained momentum as it opened, and swung back against the barn with a crash. Brian shuffled on in, and Jean pulled the door closed behind them to keep out the wind.

It was dark in the barn except for a shaft of light that came through a window above the haymow. Jean pulled her scarf down and looked around. A musty smell of cows and earth and leather filled her nostrils, and from the back of the barn came the muffled chomping and the occasional stomp of three cows and the horses.

Brian made a complete circle, staring hard at the stalls and the hay, and said simply, "I don't like it here."

Jean wasn't so sure how she felt about it herself. There was something appealing, however, in the musty solitude of the barn and the crunching of the gentle cows.

"I don't like anything," Brian went on. "I don't like the barn or the house or church or Grandmother McGinnis. Especially I don't like Grandmother."

"Well, you certainly weren't behaving yourself in church this morning," Jean told him.

"Mommy wouldn't snap my wrist," Brian said, remembering the hurt. "If Mommy was here, she wouldn't let her do it."

A hen screeched in the hay above, rising on one leg and flapping her wings triumphantly.

"Stupid old chicken," said Brian. "Stupid old barn."

There was a soft crunch of footsteps in the snow outside. Jean turned around and followed the sound with her eyes. The footsteps started near the back and came around the side and then around in front. There they stopped altogether.

Brian looked up at Jean. "Who was that?"

"I don't know. Shhhhh."

The chicken settled down again but there was no sound from outside. Suddenly the great door of the barn began to open. The wind caught it and crashed it against the side of the barn.

Jean stared. The doorway was empty. There was no one there and no sound from outside.

"Brian!" she began, but all at once there was a scraping, sliding, banging noise on the door itself. Then, silence.

"Brian! Let's go!" Jean said quickly, her mind suddenly full of the Little People that Grandmother talked about. "Somebody must have opened that door!"

"Hey! Up here!"

Jean jerked her head toward the top of the barn. There, in the window above the haymow, sat a boy about her age, grinning at them.

"Is he an elf?" Brian said, staring at the boy in the stocking cap.

"No, he's too big for that," said Jean, as though she almost believed in them herself.

The boy in the window cocked his head and sighed loudly. "Well, aren't you gonna ask me to come in?"

"You're already half in," said Jean, "so you might as well come the rest of the way. What are you doing up there anyway?"

The boy grasped the rafters with both hands, swung himself down on the hay, and slid to the floor beside Jean and Brian.

"I always come in that way," he said, brushing his hands on his jacket. "Who wants to come in a door when there's a window?"

"What do you come in here for?" Jean inquired. "Does Grandmother know you're here?"

"Well, she does and she doesn't," said the boy, standing up. His big eyes were so distinct that even the hollows around them looked blue. Jean could tell that he was quite skinny, in spite of his heavy jacket.

The boy laughed a little, showing a space where a tooth was missing. "She knows I'm about, but she doesn't know just where. I'm Tommy Pepper and I live with Donald Harvie. He's the handyman on this farm, and he told me you was comin'."

So that was how Aunt Gwen had come to know Mr. Harvie! Jean was conscious of Tommy Pepper staring at her feet and she looked down. Aunt Gwen's old boots were about four inches too long, and stuck crazily out in front of her like the feet of a clown. She blushed.

"Brother! Where'd you get your clothes?" Tommy exclaimed, looking first at Jean and then at Brian. "You must have an awful big sister!"

"I don't have a sister," said Jean. "These are Aunt Gwen's."

Tommy laughed. "You look like the moles under the chicken house. Wait till summer comes and I'll show you." He looked around. "Well, what are you going to do next, moles? Have you seen the silo yet? Come on up the haymow and I'll show you how to climb out the window and down the door."

"Jean! Jean-O!" Another voice sounded outside, and Jean went to look.

"I'm in here, Grandmother," she called as the old woman made her way along the path, milk pail in hand.

Before Jean could turn around, Tommy had scrambled up the haystack, grabbed the rafters, and swung himself to the window ledge. As soon as Grandmother came through the door, Tommy disappeared in a scramble and clatter down the side of the barn, and then all was still once more.

Grandmother dropped the pail and looked around. "Wha' was tha'?" she asked. "Did ye hear tha' noise, Jean?"

"It was an elf," said Brian. "A great big elf with a pointy hat on his head."

Grandmother looked at Jean. "Wha' did ye see? Are the Little Folk aroond? Tell the truth, noo."

Jean had to smile. "No, Grandmother. We met a boy named Tommy Pepper. He's going to show us the moles in the summer."

"Huh!" Grandmother picked up the pail and started across the barn to the cows. "Better he should show ye his parents first. Him wi' no home an' no kin, livin' off Donald Harvie like he was his son. He's a strange boy, he is, and wouldn't surprise me a bit had he an elf on his back."

Jean wasn't sure about the elf on his back, but Tommy Pepper certainly had an elfish look in his eyes, and somehow, the winter afternoon did not seem quite so dreary, just knowing that he was about.

Chapter *4*

IT WAS EVEN colder the next day. Jean sat at the big table, eating muffins and porridge and absently digging her nails in the ice on the window.

"Hurry, noo," said Grandmother, frowning at the dawdling. "If there's anythin' worse tha' bein' late to service o' a Sunday, it's bein' late to school. An' on your first day, too."

There was stomping of feet on the back porch, and Aunt Gwen came in. Her cheeks were as red as the plaid scarf around her neck, and a soft veil of snow covered her hair.

"Car won't start," she said, pushing the big gray handle of the pump up and down and filling a pail. "Guess the children will have to walk. You remember where the school is, don't you, Jean? We passed it coming home from service. A mile up the road, down the long lane on the right, past the little bridge and the pine trees."

Jean nodded. She looked out at the snow and realized she would have to wear Aunt Gwen's floppy clothes. Her own coat was much too light for weather like this.

Aunt Gwen read her thoughts. "If I can get the car running by three, I'll come for you at school and we'll stop by Shirley Aimes's house. She's a little larger than you, but her boots will fit better than mine."

When Jean and Brian were dressed once more in Aunt Gwen's old clothes, Grandmother thrust a lunch bucket in Jean's hand. "There's meat in the sandwiches today," she said. "Go straight to school an' don't get in cars wi' strangers. Do ye hear me noo, Jean?"

It had snowed again in the night, and with each step she took, Jean had to turn her toes in to keep the boots on. The icy wind took her breath away, and her eyelids hurt with the sting of the snow.

She took a deep breath and held it as she grasped Brian's mittened hand. The hill was as still as a white frosted cake, and even the wind that pelted their faces with icy bits of snow blew noiselessly. No cars disturbed the white blanket, and the sparrows which fluttered about the old rail fence hopped without chirping.

By the time they reached the crest of the hill, Jean

was warm with the climbing. Snow had fallen into the rims of her boots, however, and she could feel the wetness soaking through her stockings. Pulling Brian behind her, she rounded the corner and started down the long lane. Deep footprints in the snow ahead led to a small playground, where the swings and seesaw lay half-buried. Jean walked up the concrete steps of the school, swallowed nervously, and pushed open the door.

The hall inside smelled of books, paint, chalk, wood, and of overshoes, wool coats, and the hodge-podge of odors from crumpled lunch sacks.

The drone of spelling recitation came zigzagging down the hallway as Jean and Brian went upstairs. Then, before Jean could kick off the floppy boots, a slim wisp of a woman appeared in the doorway at the end of the hall. She looked at them over the strange half-circle glasses on her nose, then smiled and walked quickly forward.

"You must be the Jean and Brian that Miss McGinnis told me about," she said. "I'm Mrs. Tulley, and we're so happy to have you. Did you have a hard time walking in all this snow?"

Jean smiled back. "A little." She was conscious of the teacher looking at the huge boots on her feet, and hurriedly kicked them off, only to have her shoes go with them. She stooped down in her stockinged feet to pick them up.

When she looked up, she saw the silent boys and girls in the doorway at the end of the hall. They did not speak or smile, but stared intently at the new girl and her brother. There were boys as tall as the teacher herself; girls with full round figures like short grandmothers; delicate-boned children, smaller than Brian; pig-tailed girls with dark round eyes; overalled boys with missing teeth; and one or two with the crumbs of breakfast still on their cheeks.

Jean's face burned with embarrassment as she fumbled awkwardly for the wet shoes stuck inside her boots. Long wisps of hair hung down her cheeks, and Aunt Gwen's great coat covered the floor when she bent over. As she stood up again, she tripped on a corner of the coat and almost lost her balance, and a titter ran through the crowd.

Mrs. Tulley clapped her hands softly. "In your seats, please," she said, and when the children disappeared, she helped Jean out of the coat and took Brian's boots off for him. Then, sensing Jean's embarrassment, she deftly patted her hair in place and smoothed the green dress. "Now," she said, standing back and giving Jean an approving nod, "you're ready to meet the others."

The sea of faces before her was almost overwhelming as Jean walked in beside Brian and the teacher. She tried to concentrate on the display of leftover valentines around the walls as Mrs. Tulley introduced her.

"Boys and girls, this is Jean McGinnis and her brother Brian. Brian will be in first grade—right over here, dear—and Jean will be in fifth. I hope that some of you will show them around at lunch time, and include them in your games at recess."

Jean let go of Brian's hand and gingerly started down the aisle toward the empty seat in the fifth row. She had just sat down when a sudden shriek filled the small room, and Brian ran after her.

"I wanna stay with Jean!" he sobbed, terrified by the strange faces. "I wanna go home!"

There was a horrified hush at the small boy's performance, and then a ripple of laughter from the tall boys next to the windows.

Mrs. Tulley stood for a moment deciding what to do. Then she said, "I think perhaps Brian is feeling a little strange among all the new children. So today I will let him sit with his sister and share her desk. But tomorrow he will sit with his own class."

Jean both hated and loved Brian at that moment. She knew exactly how he felt, and almost wished she had a big sister herself she could run to. But his behavior only made their late entrance all the worse, and he embarrassed her so horribly that tears came to her own eyes and she desperately fought them off.

"*City.*"

The word was as plain as the answer in a spelling recitation, and Jean wondered what it meant. She turned to look at the girl on her right, only to hear it repeated from another direction.

"City . . . city . . . ," the whisper ran as it traveled up and down the rows.

City. She could tell by the way they said it. City children were not exactly prized out here in the great white country around Oshkosh, where the snow was several feet deep and the winds howled. Here, the children not only got to school on winter mornings, but got there on time. And now, with an aunt's old clothes and a crybaby brother, Jean felt herself the center of attention, as eyes focussed her way, hands covered mouths, and the derisive whisper went its rounds.

She felt like leaping up and telling them that she wasn't from the city at all, just a small coal mining town out east. But somehow she knew it wouldn't make any difference. "City" meant anything different, and that certainly meant her.

And then, a finger poked her shoulder, and a quiet voice said softly, "Hi, moles."

Jean turned her head and stared into the twinkly blue eyes of Tommy Pepper.

At a quarter of twelve, Jean and Brian filed out to the hallway with the other children, taking their lunch bucket to the basement room below. The fireplace on one side was lit, and the pupils pulled the benches closer to it.

Tommy Pepper sat on top of a table with a row

of boys, all swinging their legs and taking big quick bites from their thick sandwiches. Jean found a space on a bench against the wall and sat down. Opening the blue lunch pail, she wordlessly handed her brother a sandwich.

"Do we have to come back tomorrow?" Brian asked miserably.

"Yes," said Jean, her lips tight.

"Do I have to sit all by myself tomorrow?"

"Yes, and you'd better not cry, either," Jean replied. "You embarrassed me. Everyone was looking."

Someone sat down on the other side of her, and Jean turned around. The girl had long, reddish brown hair which had been pushed back from her face with a white band. She wore a white blouse and a blue skirt that matched her stockings. She was, Jean decided, the best-dressed girl in the school.

"Hi," said the girl, carefully unwrapping a package of cupcakes. "I'm Shirley Aimes. Mother told me you were coming to live with your aunt." She took a bite, savoring the white filling inside the dark cake.

"Hi." Jean picked at the bread crumbs in her lap, wondering what to say to the pretty girl.

"You're from the city, aren't you?" Shirley asked.

Jean squirmed. Why did they have to make her seem so different? "Not really. Logan's just a small town."

"Oh. Then you're not country or city. You're just sort of nothing." Shirley gave a little laugh and tossed her cellophane wrapper into the fireplace. "Well, next year we won't be going to a country school any more. They're building a big township school over on the new highway, and a bus will come around to pick us up. Isn't that great?"

"I suppose so," said Jean. "I don't know where we'll be living then. After Daddy gets here, we're going to move into a house of our own, and I don't know where it will be."

"Maybe you'll even move away," said Shirley. "I wish we would. I wish we'd move right into the center of Oshkosh. I wouldn't mind being 'city' at all. I really wouldn't."

"Why?" Jean asked, looking at her carefully.

Shirley shrugged and started to answer, but Mrs. Tulley blew her whistle for games, and everyone got in a circle.

"You'll see," Shirley said, and they all took hands.

There was arithmetic in the afternoon, and history and writing. When the big clock on the wall chimed three, books and tablets were whisked away and all six grades swarmed to the hall to dress for the cold journey home.

Jean hung back, waiting until the others had gone. She found Brian's boots and coat and slowly helped him dress. When she could delay no longer, she reached for the great coat and the huge boots of Aunt Gwen's.

Suddenly, the boots began walking away with the

coat above them. As Jean and Brian and Mrs. Tulley stared, the boots clomped about the hall in a circle, and the loose arms of the great coat flopped crazily back and forth.

Then, just as suddenly, the old gray boots and coat went back to the coat rack. There was a scurrying sound from somewhere inside them, and out stepped Tommy Pepper, grinning with his strange blue eyes and wide mouth.

"Tommy!" Jean said aghast, and started to laugh. "I almost thought. . ."

"I know," said Tommy, rolling his eyes. "The Little People."

Mrs. Tulley shook her head. "Tommy Pepper is always up to something!" she said, half disapprovingly, but there was a grin in her voice that sent Tommy prancing friskily out the door where he disappeared in the snow like a nimble elf.

Aunt Gwen's car was waiting at the end of the lane. As Jean climbed inside, she found Shirley Aimes in the back seat. "We're going to stop at Shirley's, so I'm giving her a ride too," Aunt Gwen said. "Hop in, Brian." The car started slowly down the country road, the engine whining. "Well, how did it go?"

"Oh, pretty good," answered Jean, hesitating.

"Except for Brian," said Shirley. "He cried."

Aunt Gwen looked sideways at Brian. He sat with his head tilted back, Grandfather's pipe dangling from his lips in forced bravado. Aunt Gwen smiled but said nothing more.

Jean felt uncomfortable beside Shirley. With her clothes, Shirley should be the most popular girl in school, but it hadn't seemed that way. She wished they were getting clothes from someone else. What if Shirley told everybody the number of dresses Jean had, and the shape they were in, about the shoes with the paper stuffed in the toes, and the stockings with darned heels?

The car came to a crunching stop in front of a tall yellow house with brown shutters. Behind it rose a yellow barn and silo. The great expanse of white fields was surrounded, as far as Jean could see, by a well-kept painted brown fence. It was a handsome farm, and a big one, and the beautifully curved railing leading up the steps to the front door told Jean that the inside of the house would be nicer still. Brian stayed in the yard to play, and Shirley took Jean and Aunt Gwen inside.

"Mother! Jean's here for the clothes!" There was something about the way Shirley said it, not impolitely, but in an offhand manner as though she gave away her slightly used dresses every day.

A woman's heels sounded on the polished floors, and a lady with large green earrings in her ears appeared in the doorway.

"Hello, Gwendolyn," she said in a friendly voice. "So this is Jean!"

"Yes, this is my niece, and here are the two dozen eggs you ordered," Aunt Gwen said, handing her the cartons.

"Come on upstairs to Shirley's bedroom and we'll see what we have," Mrs. Aimes called over her shoulder, leading the way. "They're nothing fancy, but I can't see throwing them out when Shirley's worn them so little."

When they reached the bedroom at the head of the stairs, Jean stopped in amazement. It was a beautiful bedroom, with a huge white ruffled canopy over the bed. There were matching curtains at the windows, and a pink velvet chair in one corner. As she turned slowly around, she saw a desk and chair with a white reading lamp, a fancy dresser covered with stuffed dogs, and there, against the wall, was a most fantastic dollhouse.

Made of plastic, its walls and porch looked like white brick, and its red roof had double chimneys for fireplaces at both ends. There were lights in the ceilings, shutters at the windows, carpets on the floor, and exquisite furniture in every room—antiqued pianos, refrigerator, china cupboard, and baby cradles.

"Shirley!" Jean breathed. "I've never seen anything like this!"

Shirley sat down on the bed, kicking off her shoes. "Mother and Daddy gave it to me once for Christmas," she said. "See. The lights come on when you press this switch. And the water in the bathtub really runs."

Jean stooped down beside the dollhouse. "Oh, Aunt Gwen, isn't it beautiful?"

"I'm glad someone appreciates it," said Mrs. Aimes. "Shirley's only played with it four times."

"I never had the right dolls," Shirley protested. "You know none of mine fit the beds."

"So now you need a whole family of dolls, and after that a wardrobe for each, and heaven knows what all," Mrs. Aimes said, laughing. "You girls have minds that flit from one thing to another."

She opened the closet and took out a large box of clothes. Aunt Gwen sat down to examine them, holding them up to Jean to check the shoulder width or the length. There was a corduroy jumper and a green print blouse, a taffeta party dress with a stain on one side, and a blue wool skirt with a button missing. There was a coat and a jacket and a pair of red boots, and a half dozen sweaters besides. Jean mechanically raised her arms and lowered them as Aunt Gwen did the measuring. She could not take her eyes off the exquisite house.

"You don't know how grateful we are," Aunt Gwen said, folding the clothes carefully and placing them back in the box. "This will be a real saving for her parents."

"I'm glad we had so much to make do," Mrs. Aimes said. "Shirley doesn't wear half her clothes, and relatives keep sending. No sense wasting, I always say."

Aunt Gwen stood up to leave. Slowly Jean put

back the small table she was holding. She flicked off the lights on the little white brick veranda, closed the French doors to the miniature dining room, and went slowly down the stairs behind Shirley, her feet drifting noiselessly on the rich carpet.

"You could come by after school tomorrow and play," Shirley said.

"Piano lessons, dear," her mother reminded, and Shirley frowned.

"I'll come back some day when you're not busy," Jean promised. "Thanks a lot."

Brian came racing across the yard, kicking up snow behind him, and they got in the car. All the way home Jean thought about the dollhouse. She could not imagine one girl getting anything as lovely as that, all for herself. How she would care for it if it were hers! She would give parties in the little house, with a miniature birthday cake and presents. She would have robberies and fires, chases and rescues. She would have a cat that slept on the piano and a dog that barked at the stars. She would have fudge parties, Christmas trees, weddings, and people falling downstairs. She would do everything in that miniature house that she would have wanted to do in a house of her own. She realized, with dismay, that she wanted more than just enough clothes, enough food, and enough money so as not to feel different. Now it was a dollhouse too. She wished for an exquisite, expensive dollhouse like Shirley's.

"What is it, Jean?" asked Aunt Gwen when they got home. "Is it the dollhouse that's on the mind?"

Jean smiled a little and nodded.

"It was pretty," said Aunt Gwen. She brought the car to a stop and let Brian jump out. "It wouldn't be quite the same, but we could always make a dollhouse."

"Make one!" said Jean. "How?"

Aunt Gwen took her down to the cellar and rummaged through the pile of boxes and kindling until she found three heavy wooden pear boxes, divided in the middle, and stood them up on end, side by side.

"To make a wee moon," Aunt Gwen began, "we need three sturdy boxes and a hundred odds and ends. There's paint in the barn and cloth in the sewing basket, and it will be the perfect thing to work on these cold evenings while we wait for spring."

Jean stared at the dirty rough boxes with the nails sticking out the ends and the splinters along the edges. She would rather have nothing at all than so crude a dollhouse. Why, Aunt Gwen actually believed you could make anything at all, even a small moon, if you tried hard enough.

Jean forced a smile and started up the stairs with a box while Aunt Gwen followed with the other two, whistling. At least it would give her aunt something to do. But Jean knew she wouldn't like it. Not after she'd seen Shirley's.

Chapter **5**

BRIAN SAT ALONE the next day, and Jean wore clothes that fit her. Still, the low whisper traveled up and down the rows, "City . . . city . . . city. . . ." When Brian bumped his knee and cried, they said it. When Jean tried to get the lid off the paste jar and couldn't, they said it. "City" was another word for "sissy," for "new," for "different," and the children said it solemnly, without smiling, as if Jean and her red-cheeked brother were intruding in a place they shouldn't be. But after several days, it didn't bother Jean quite so much.

The snowy hill to the school was just as hard to climb as ever. When the day was over, however, Jean and Brian would race to begin the long descent, using the slick car tracks as a slide if the road were empty.

At the bottom, before the road grew flat again, they would stop at the huge round drainage tunnel under the road. Jean would get on one side and Brian on the other, and they would shout back and forth from opposite ends of the big pipe. Sometimes, for a few brief moments, Tommy Pepper would slide along behind them, the wind blowing the tassel of his cap out behind him. And then he would be gone, running on ahead on top the rail fence, or leaping out over the snowy fields, zigzagging this way and that until finally he was only a small black bug on the white of the fields.

The following week, Aunt Gwen started work on the dollhouse. It was fun, Jean decided, to scrounge up things: a square of old linoleum which Aunt Gwen cut with a razor blade to the exact shape of the little kitchen, some odds and ends of wallpaper which papered the entire living room in stripes, and a green and yellow flower print for one of the bed spreads. Corks made excellent bases for the kitchen table and chairs, and Grandmother brought in a white shingle from the barn, which she painstakingly cut into tops for the kitchenette set. Small empty spools became furniture in other rooms, and every night Jean and her aunt sat in front of the big fireplace and painted another wall of the dollhouse, or carpeted a floor, or sawed out a window, or hung a new pair of curtains on a toothpick rod. And bit by bit, it began to look different.

Jean said nothing more about Shirley's dollhouse. She wasn't quite so sure about it now. She wasn't even sure she wanted an antique piano or a tub with running water. Instead, she silently watched Aunt Gwen's big freckled hands working on a new idea, and stood back with her to ooh and ah when something new was added.

"You know," said Jean as she carefully painted the bathroom walls yellow, "I'm really too old for dollhouses."

"So am I," her aunt chuckled, "but I'm having such a good time!"

"We could say it's a dream house," Jean suggested. "I mean, we don't have to have dolls or anything."

"A dream house is fine," said Aunt Gwen. "We'll make it just the kind of house we'd like to have ourselves."

On Friday, after school, Brian was out in the pasture chasing the colt through the snow, and Jean had stepped inside the three-walled tractor shed to get out of the wind. Against the back wall, turkeys nestling in makeshift roosts stared at her beadily. A brown mouse scurried along a rake hanging on the wall and disappeared into a corner, but Patches, hunched up on one wheel of the tractor, ignored it.

"Hello."

Jean turned around. Nothing. Instinctively she looked up. There was Tommy Pepper, hanging upside down from the roof of the shed.

"For goodness sake!" said Jean. "Do you always

come down into houses instead of through doors?"

Tommy Pepper swung himself down and landed on his feet in the snow. "What door? Shed don't even have a door."

Jean laughed. "But you could have walked in on the ground. Why do you always drop in, like falling out of an airplane or something?"

"Not an airplane," said Tommy, crawling up on the tractor and thrusting his red hands in his pockets. "Out of the sky. That's what your granny tells everybody."

"Why would Grandmother go around saying you fell out of the sky?"

"The blue, then," said Tommy. He wrinkled up his nose, lowered his voice, and imitated Grandmother McGinnis: "That Pepper boy! Out of the blue he came, and into Donald Harvie's kitchen where he's been eatin' ever since!"

Jean looked at him curiously. "Well, how did you happen to live with Donald Harvie?"

"I don't really live with him. I sleep in his house, and I eat at his table, but I don't really belong there." He stopped and tried to make a silly face, but somehow it didn't come off. "I'm just visitin' for a year till my Pa gits back this way with the carnival. He's gonna pay Mr. Harvie a hunnert dollars for my keep. I heard him tell."

"Is your mother with the carnival too?"

"She ain't alive. Pa's my family, but Mr. Harvie

says I ought to have steady schoolin', and Pa didn't say no."

"Why doesn't Grandmother like you?"

Tommy's eyes grew even wider and a grin spread to his ears. "She thinks I'm a goblin."

"How could she think that?"

The skinny boy shrugged his shoulders, bony even under his jacket. "I don't know. But I come in the barn onct when she was milkin', and she jerked around so she knocked over the pail. Weren't me that knocked it over or scairt the cow or fell off the milkin' stool, but she turned me out. Said never set foot inside again."

"So you come in head first," Jean laughed, blowing on her fingers to keep them warm. "I don't think she believes you're a goblin, though."

"Okay." Tommy Pepper folded his arms across his chest. "I dare you to go in the house and say, 'Granny, Tommy Pepper's here and wants a ginger cookie.' If she gives it to you, I'll jump off the barn."

Jean smiled. "Wait here."

She trudged across the snowy yard to the back porch and opened the door to the kitchen. Grandmother was lifting a pan of steaming potatoes which she dumped with a grunt in the sink.

"Grandmother," Jean called from the doorway. "Tommy Pepper's here and wants a ginger cookie."

The pan clattered out of Grandmother's hands and rolled across the floor.

"Here?" she cried. "In this house?"

Jean stared at the old lady. "No. He's in the tractor shed."

"Tell him to go right on," Grandmother said, waving her apron at Jean. "Go right on. Ye feed him a cookie in the tractor shed, an' he'll be eatin' apples in the barn. Once in the barn and he'll be in the house a' the table. The boy's got an elf on his back, an' the Little People will be movin' in sure as Tommy Pepper sets foot in the kitchen."

Jean could hardly believe it. "Can I have a cookie for Brian and myself?" she asked.

Grandmother grunted again and lifted the lid of the cookie crock, giving Jean two cookies and no more. She was still mumbling when Jean closed the door.

Tommy Pepper stared openmouthed when he saw Jean coming. "She *did*?"

"Not really," Jean said, giving him both cookies. "She doesn't think you're a goblin. She thinks you've an elf on your back."

Tommy greedily ate the cookies in four big bites. "She's nuts."

"She is not," said Jean defensively, regretting the cookies a little. "She's superstitious, that's all. The old folks believe these things in Scotland."

"She ever tell you about the kelpies?" Tommy said. "Ask her about 'em sometime. Donald Harvie never comes over but she's tellin' him about the kelpies."

"Jean-O!" came Grandmother's voice. "Jean-O!

Brian! The supper's waitin'."

"Anyway," said Jean, "come back again. Maybe she won't care so much if we stay outside."

Tommy shrugged and watched Jean go. "Ask her about the kelpies," he called. "That's the best of all."

A letter came from Jean's father. He had sold the little house in Logan, and he and Mother would be driving to Oshkosh as soon as they could get packed. Jean could scarcely wait.

It did not snow again, but the March wind seemed to cut through the walls of the two-story house. Each night Jean stayed in front of the fire as long as Grandmother would allow it.

One evening, as the old woman sat sewing the great yellow quilt on her lap, her shaggy white eyebrows squeezed between her glasses and the wrinkles on her forehead, Jean saw her glance at the clock and said hurriedly, to stall her, "Grandmother, what's a kelpie?"

Grandmother McGinnis paused with her needle in midair. "Why do ye ask, lass?"

"Tommy Pepper said you knew all about them."

"Humph." Grandmother's needle worked in and out again, and her white brows came together in a frown. "The boy knows more tha' he ought of a Scottish farm, an' he'd best tend to the elf on his own back afore he looks for a kelpie."

"But what is a kelpie? Have you ever seen one?"

For a moment Grandmother did not answer. The

fire crackled, a mouse scurried in the wall, and finally Grandmother put her needle down again and examined the sewing she had done. "Aye," she said. "I ha'e seen a kelpie."

Jean's eyes opened wide. "Where?"

"It was a long time ago," said Grandmother, "when I was a girl on the Isle of Skye. One night my sister an' I had gone doon to the water to fetch home the cows tha' were swimmin' back from the pasture islands. We had got halfway up the hill an' my sister was ahead o' me, when sudden I heard a faint soond, like someone callin' my name, an' I turned aroond to see a gray horse, far oot in the water, an' he was lookin' at me an' his tail was switchin'."

Across the room, Aunt Gwen's magazine rustled impatiently. "But, Mother, your sister didn't see it."

"Aye, tha's true, an' tha's wha' makes it proof. T'was seen only to me, an' wi' my own two eyes I saw it clear."

"You admitted it was a foggy night," said Aunt Gwen.

"Aye, but not too foggy to see where the horse was standin'. 'Maggie, Maggie,' the horse calls, its eyes flashin' like it was impatient to be off. 'Maggie, Maggie,' an' I took a step doon the hill to see it better."

Jean hugged her knees tightly and shivered. Grandmother sat motionless, her eyes half-closed, her fingers locked tightly together.

"Then," said Grandmother slowly, "I tripped. I

60

fell an' rolled halfway doon the hill an' my sister ran after me. When she caught up wi' me, my face was white as a new-bought sheet, she said, an' when we looked oot o'er the water again, the horse was gone. T'was then I knew it to be a kelpie."

Jean sat scarcely breathing as the big clock on the wall ticked on. Finally, when it looked as though the old lady might be falling asleep, Jean touched her lightly on the arm and said, "What would have happened, Grandmother, if you hadn't tripped?"

Grandmother McGinnis opened her eyes. "Then, I would ha'e gone to the river, an' climbed on the horse, an' it would ha'e taken me doon below the water, the last the world would ha'e seen o' me."

The shadows on the wall seemed monstrously large, and the fire in the hearth looked like two dancing horses, their manes aflame. When Patches rose suddenly and stretched, Jean jumped with fright.

"Now, Mother," said Aunt Gwen, dropping her magazine on the floor. "You're going to scare her to death. This is America, not Scotland."

"There's a river here too," said Grandmother. "Kelpies go where the Scottish go, an' I'm only tellin' wha' she ought to know."

"Kelpies or not, the river's a good place to swim in the summer." Aunt Gwen stood up and looked at the clock. "Come on, Jean, it's long past your bedtime."

As Jean climbed the stairs to the cold room above, she wondered what Grandmother had looked like as a girl. Perhaps she was tall and blond like Aunt Gwen, instead of bent and fat as she was now. She wondered what Grandmother felt now that her husband was buried and she was here in the new land with no one to believe in the Little People but herself.

"Does it worry you, Jean? The kelpies?" Aunt Gwen asked, pulling off her orange sweater and reaching for her robe.

"That's not all she talks about," Jean said. "There are other things, too."

Aunt Gwen smiled and nodded as she brushed out her hair. "Yes. There are witches in the trees and kelpies in the river and a garden full of Little People, just waiting to come up from their home underground and move in with the family. That's why she keeps the house locked up so tight on a full moon. And if you watch when she's baking, you'll see her put a bit of dough aside, in case there are any Little Folk about the kitchen. So as to get in good with them, you know. But you'll get used to it, honey. Besides, what would we talk about on cold winter nights if it weren't for Grandmother's stories?"

Jean giggled and snuggled down further under the covers, scrunching up her toes on the cold sheets. Kelpies indeed!

It was a bleak afternoon. Even the sun had a dirty gray look. The wind blew in great gusts, whipping Jean's coat about her legs. Back in Logan, the snow would be gone by now, and here and there a small wild flower would be peeping up through the frozen ground. But here in the north, there was nothing but tired old snow, a gray sky, and dead crackling tree branches which bespoke of elves and witches and the Little People that lived under the garden.

As Jean and Brian reached the bottom of the hill on their way home from school, a car sounded behind them, and Jean pulled Brian off onto the shoulder to let it pass. Instead, however, the car stopped, and Jean's heart quickened as she went on, not daring to stop or turn around. She remembered Grandmother's admonitions about talking to strangers, and hurried on faster, wondering if Aunt Gwen were watching from the kitchen window.

Then, out of the corner of her eye, Jean could see a man getting out of the car behind them.

"Run, Brian!" she whispered, terrified. "Hurry!"

They began to run, clumping clumsily along in their boots.

"Hey!" yelled the man. "Hey!" And suddenly he was coming after them, leaping down into the ditch and gaining with every step, swooping after them like a big black eagle.

"Brian!" Jean screamed. "Run! Run!"

Suddenly the man's arms reached out and grabbed Brian. And then, above his shrieking, Jean heard the man say, "Brian, Brian, it's me, lad."

Jean wheeled around, almost losing her balance,

and suddenly she was rushing up to the eagle and throwing her arms around its neck and almost crying.

"Daddy! I didn't know it was you! I didn't know you were here!"

And the next moment the big round head, so much like Jean's, with the dark blond hair and the wisps of eyebrows, was snuggled against hers. Two big arms were hugging her tight and lifting her off the ground.

"Daddy! Daddy!" Brian cried gaily, trying to climb up too, and the big man started hugging them all over again.

They walked back to the car, all hugging together like a six-legged bird, and Jean gave another squeal. For the dark bundle of old fur coat in the front seat could only be Mother, and Jean flung herself on her lap before she could even see her face. Two tiny hands reached out from the ball of fur and hugged her tightly.

How silly, Jean kept saying to herself. I didn't cry at all when we left Logan. And now that Mother is here...

In a few minutes Mother's dark eyes were searching Jean's, and her tiny mouth was smiling. Her small, heart-shaped face with the high cheekbones looked all pink and shiny with the cold. "Jean," she said, "has it been so bad? Really?"

Jean couldn't answer because the stupid tears were still coming, and Brian was scrambling up her back to get to Mother. Finally the car began to move on down the road to the farmhouse, with all four of the family squeezed in the front seat, everyone babbling at once.

Chapter 6

ANGUS MCGINNIS was an enormous man. As Jean watched him across the breakfast table, smearing each pancake with yellow butter, she thought of him as a gentle giant. The hair on his head and his brows and arms was so light and so fine that one had to look hard to see it at all, and his great ears looked almost pink and tender, like a baby's cheek.

His voice, however, was deep, and when he said, "Pass the syrup, lass," Jean's hands moved quickly to slide the big blue pitcher toward his plate.

Further down the table sat Mother, wrapped up tight in a rose flannel robe, as small as Father was big. Her short dark hair was all curly around her face, and her little pointed chin stuck out from beneath the coffee cup she lifted now and then to her lips.

It was Grandmother who was doing all the talking.

" 'Tis a poorly done farm wi'oot a man to keep it,"
she said, scraping a pan of steaming porridge into a
big bowl in the center of the table. She banged the
spoon and waddled back to the stove. "Thirteen
months Gwen an' I been hoein' and milkin' since your
faither died, Angus, an' it isn't fit for a Scottish lady
to be leavin' her kitchen. There's work in the house
tha's wastin'."

Father drank a gulp of coffee before answering.
"What about Donald Harvie? I thought he was hired
to do the heavy chores."

Grandmother grunted. "Him? He's a poor excuse
for a farmer. Slow as a duck goin' to roost, an' talkin'
so soft I cannot hear him. Don't know i' he's talkin'
for or again' me."

Jean glanced at Aunt Gwen just in time to see her
hide a smile.

"Well, the place looks pretty good to me," big
Angus said. "Walk shoveled, hay in, silo filled, and
the man's got his own cottage to tend as well."

"His cottage an' an elf on his back," Grandmother
said. "He's half a brain in his head, for he's taken on
a waif from the carnival people to school till the show
comes back this way."

"I can't see the harm in that." There was a sharp-
ness now in Aunt Gwen's voice, and the smile was
gone. "It's a lot more charity in the heart to take the
boy than to turn him out."

"As if 'twere doin' the lad a mite o' good," said

Grandmother. "If he learns Donald Harvie's slow ways on top his own, the boy won't be worth two pennies."

"It wasn't anybody but Donald Harvie kept us with kindlin' all winter, and that wasn't a job we set him to do," Aunt Gwen snapped, her eyes flashing. And suddenly she got up from the table, clunked down her coffee cup, and took the morning paper out onto the sun porch.

Jean stared. It was the first time she had seen her aunt upset.

"It's dairy farmin' I've come for, Mother. You know that," Jean's father said determinedly. He was eating slower now, choosing his words carefully. "I want to make my own start. That's what I got my heart set on, and bein' handed a farm and cattle don't have the same feelin' about it."

" 'Tis a birthright!" Grandmother declared. " 'Twas your faither's farm, an' who should get it but his son?"

"It was always a needlin' point between us, too," said Angus. "He wanted me to go it with him, but he wanted crops and I wanted a dairy. You know how he felt when I moved to Logan. You know how two years went by not even writin'. Now that he's gone, I don't figure to step in and take what he built up himself. It's more Gwen's. She's the one should have it. She's put in the work."

"Then ye share it, the two o' ye," said Grandmother,

plopping down exasperatedly on a stool by the stove. "Your faither's soul don't bear ye no grudge for goin' off like tha', mistake or no. He knew it were not goin' well for ye, but he didn't glory on it. Is there a reason a big house like this should go half lived in?"

Big Angus continued to eat. Mother jerked nervously at her napkin, wiping each finger separately, and said, "It's just that Angus has always had his heart set on his own farm, and I've wanted a little house of my own."

"Wi' all the added expense!" scoffed Grandmother. "Wha's become o' the frugality, Angus, since we left Skye? Wha's the sense o' four grown people in two houses? Never di' I hear such nonsense! Ye ha'e a house an' job in Logan an' couldna' make a go o' it. Wha' makes ye think a house an' dairy. . ."

"It wasn't my fault about the job, Mother," said Angus. "No one knew the mines would lay off that many men. Luke had always made a go of it before."

" 'Tis a poor friend tha' talks a man into packin' up his family, crossin' the country, an' settlin' doon in a dirty coal toon to take to a mine wi' only four years o' life left."

"He couldn't have known that, Mother. No one did. Now I want me a dairy farm, and I got a bit o' money from my house to pay down on a small place here. First I've got to find me a job."

Grandmother swished down off the stool and stalked angrily to the sink. At the same time, Mother and Father got up from the table and left the room. Jean and Brian were alone in the kitchen with Grandmother, and Brian's tricks with his fork and spoon did not help matters. Grandmother had her back to the table when Brian's fork flipped out of his hand, flew across the room, struck the yellow teapot hanging at the window with ivy growing in it, and sent the plant and teapot crashing to the floor.

Grandmother did not see the fork which had caused it all. She saw only the broken teapot and the dirt and the ivy and the door to the back porch that Angus had gone out and left open.

She jerked around, clutching at her wool shawl, and stared wide-eyed at the floor. Suddenly she rushed over and slammed the door shut, her hand trembling.

"The Little Folk are movin' in," she breathed, "an' noo the tricks are upon us!"

Spring came to the farm. The snow on the roof of the barn slid off in sheets, and the icicles under the eaves dripped steadily before they fell crackling onto the soggy ground below. There was a fresh smell in the air that the cattle noticed, and they stomped at the big door of the barn, impatient to be out and across the fields.

The pig had a litter of young, which ran rooting and squealing about the pen. Jean and Brian loved to climb up on the fence and watch them push through the mud to the slop trough and back again to the warm, coarse body of the sow.

Patches, too, had a litter, and most of the kittens had her trademark, a patch of white on each paw. They rolled and frolicked about the yard in the sunshine, and delighted Brian by chasing the string he dangled from his pocket.

It was a good time, Jean decided, going out with Grandmother one early May morning to plant sweet peas by the side of the house. Father had found work on a dairy farm on the outskirts of the city, and he and Mother were looking around for a little farm of their own.

"I guess it won't be long till we're leaving," Jean said, squatting down beside the big woman and helping poke the seeds into the ground with her finger.

"An' where d'ye guess ye'll be goin'?" Grandmother said, puffing as she pushed the dirt over the seeds. "Will ye sleep in the barn, lass?"

"Of course not," said Jean. "Daddy will buy us a house. We'll still come to visit all the time, though."

"Aye, an' eat wi' us too, for there won't be money for house an' groceries too, I'll guess. Ye cannot buy the moon wi' a paper bag. It'll not do to think on things ye cannot afford."

"But I heard him tell Mother he was trying," Jean insisted. "Maybe by fall, he said."

"Tha' girl!" said Grandmother. "Tha' girl your faither married 'ud ha'e him tryin' for a silver egg from a gold hen."

Jean frowned. "Aunt Gwen says, to make a wee moon, all you need is a wee bit of patience and a lot of hard work."

"Aunt Gwen," Grandmother declared huffily, getting up and limping back to the house again, "has rhubarb in her head."

Grandmother didn't like anybody that day, Jean decided, for once inside the kitchen she banged the cupboard doors and looked positively ferocious. "There's trouble all aboot," she said. "The teapot boiled dry an' almost burned through, my needle disappeared from under my nose, the cat had a fit for no reason, an' my blue china vegetable bowl fell doon off the shelf. The Little Folk are a' aroond us, an' will be takin' over both the house an' the barn i' we're not careful."

School was not improved by the coming of spring. In some ways it was worse. Recess no longer took place in the basement but out on the big soft grounds that stretched down the hill to the river. The boys weren't permitted to go to the river, but they went anyway, sneaking back with snakes and water bugs which they dropped in the girls' lunch pails or set on the backs of their necks.

Jean hated recess, and clung close to the building when she saw the boys coming. She hated lunch time even more, for that was longer. She would sit near the door, her lunch bucket opened on her lap, engulfed in the familiar aroma of home-baked bread heavily smeared with peanut butter, hard-boiled eggs, carrots, and perhaps a sugared doughnut. Brian was getting bolder. He'd made his peace with the boys in his own grade, and even got on good terms with the second-grade bully. So now he no longer tagged after his sister, and sometimes Jean almost wished he would.

The quiet heckling never stopped. If anyone else tripped going up the steps, no one seemed to notice. But if Jean did, the snickering was immediate. If she made a mistake in recitation, the grins were obvious. She felt as though the class rejoiced in any misfortune which befell her. They mimicked her slight accent which was a strange mixture of Scotch and West Virginian. And they still called her *city*. She was the only new girl in the school for the last four years and the only one who hadn't been born in this great northern farm country. Only Shirley Aimes and Tommy Pepper left her alone.

It was strange about Shirley, Jean decided, watching the chestnut-haired girl sitting sideways in the swing at lunch time, slowly dragging her foot in the sand. Shirley didn't seem to have any more friends than she did. Shirley Aimes, who lived in the big yellow farmhouse with the fancy fence and barn, whose family bought eggs from the McGinnises rather than raise their own chickens, who had hired help to take care of both the fields and the house. "A real gentleman farmer," Grandmother called Shirley's father, which meant well-to-do.

No one really teased Shirley. No one mimicked her or tripped her or hid her lunch box. But no one sat with her either, or chose her first for volley ball. Shirley walked home alone each day to practice her piano lessons or her ballet lessons or singing. The truth was, as everyone knew, that even if someone had walked home with Shirley, she wouldn't have been allowed to play. For Shirley's life outside of school consisted of all the refinements and schedules and activities that often filled the lives of city children, and Shirley's mother thought nothing of driving her daughter into Oshkosh several times a week for lessons. And because Jean remained friendly with her, and sat and talked with her when she could, the class took its annoyance with Shirley out on Jean, for Jean had no wealthy family to back her up, and it was safer to tackle a McGinnis than an Aimes.

And then one day it happened. One horrible day that had started out usual enough, with a history test and a spelling bee, and Mrs. Tulley reading the next to the last chapter of *Tom Sawyer*. Now, as the three o'clock bell sounded, Jean gathered up her homework and her sweater and started down the lane with the others. Brian had long since disappeared over the fields on the heels of Tommy Pepper.

She had almost reached the road beyond the bridge, when suddenly one of the older boys came rushing back toward the others, his face red with running.

"Hey! Come on!" he yelled excitedly. "On up

ahead . . . a guy just told me . . . some truck ran into a cow. There's blood all over the road! Come on!"

The boys in the group started to run, but turned around to see if the girls were coming. "Come on, Lu Ann. Come on, Hildy!"

The girls buzzed excitedly among themselves. Did they dare go look at the dead animal? They knew they would go, yet they dreaded it.

"Come on, you're chicken!" the boys yelled, urging them on.

An older girl in a green dress looked around at the others. "Are you really going?" she said, and her eye caught Jean's. "Jean, are you going?"

It was the only sort of invitation Jean had had from the other girls. The boys looked at her too.

"Well, you going?"

"Sure," said Jean. "Why not?"

"Hey, she's going! Jean's going!" she heard a boy say, a note of respect in his voice. "Well, what about the rest of you?"

"We're going," said the big girl in the green dress. They crowded close to Jean as if for assurance. "Did you ever see a hit cow?"

"No," said Jean. "Did you?"

The girl shook her head, and for a brief minute they shared a look of empathy, each comforting the other. She was in! She was going! Jean was almost leading the way, following so surefooted behind the boys. City, was she?

As they turned onto the road they saw Shirley standing there.

"What's all the excitement?" Shirley called.

"Cow got hit up the road a piece," the boy told her. "We're gonna go see."

"Oh, you're not!" Shirley recoiled as if she herself had touched it. She stared aghast at Jean and the other girls as they turned off in the direction of the accident. "Jean! You're not!"

"Sure she is!" said the boy. "We all are. Come on. You're chicken."

"I am not!" said Shirley defensively. "I would, but we're going away."

"Yeah," said the boy, laughing to himself. "Yeah, sure."

"We are!" said Shirley, her face red as she witnessed the whole class turning up the road.

Jean immediately noticed the flush on her face, the derision of the boys, the quiet snickers of the girls, and for the first time since she had come to Oshkosh, it was she who was on the other side of the fence. It was she, Jean, who stood in the crowd and snickered at someone else. Suddenly she placed one hand simperingly up to her face and said mockingly, "She would, she *really* would, but she's just *got* to practice her piano lessons!"

The laughter was instantaneous. It welled up deep from the big-footed boys. It came rippling and gushing from the high-voiced girls. It rolled out over the road where Shirley was standing and on across the fields, a pent-up laughter that burst through like a torrential rainfall.

For a moment Jean wallowed in the laughter. It surged around her, carrying her along with it, slapping her back and pulsing her forehead. She was *in!* For the moment she was really, truly an insider sharing a private joke.

And then, just as suddenly, she felt all the agony that the girl was suffering there alone. She was standing on the shoulder of the road as the others passed by, her face crimson, her throat tight, her eyes small with the sting of the hurt. For a moment Jean felt she could not move. She could not possibly leave until she'd said something to gloss it over, to show Shirley she really hadn't meant it. But the others were moving on and she was moving with them. The smile was still on her face as her heart sank inside her, and she dared not look back.

She was part of the group as they moved down the road, and yet she wasn't. She saw and exclaimed over the carcass on the road, and yet her thoughts were back on Shirley. Then, as a truck rumbled by, it splattered the cow's blood, and Jean could feel it splash on her legs.

As she looked down, she saw Shirley's blue skirt, the prettiest of the lot, and suddenly she was bending over the grass throwing up, her stomach retching. She was part of the group no longer.

Jean counted the days till school closed. She was more of an outsider now than she was before. She avoided Shirley's eyes, and the dark-haired girl, in turn, said nothing to her. As for the other children, Jean isolated herself from them all. It would have been easy to put the blame on them. She could say that what she had said to Shirley they had been thinking for years and years. But it was she, not the others, who had dealt the blow, and she could not stand herself for it. Her studies improved greatly, for she even spent her recess periods tucked away on the steps with a book. But she could not bear to wear any of the clothes Shirley had given her, even though it meant finishing out the last few weeks with only three dresses.

It was hard, however, to ignore the May sunshine. Jean's mother, too, had a touch of spring fever which kept her outside the house whenever she could think of a reason. It wasn't difficult, because Grandmother wanted things done just so. She wanted to do the dishes herself, the cooking herself, the dusting and mending, and felt that Rita had enough to do just taking care of the children and keeping out of her way. So young Mrs. McGinnis stayed outdoors as much as she could, pulling up a weed here and there, gathering the eggs, and feeding the chickens.

One afternoon, Jean and her mother went out in the pasture to see the colt. Jean carried one of the kittens in her arms, stroking its soft fluff with her hand, and playfully draping it over her arm like a fur piece. They crossed the clover field to the fence where a row of plum trees moved their pink blossoms in a soft ballet.

They sat up on the fence, drinking in the sun, while the mare trotted over, her colt behind. She looked them over, nuzzled the colt, then bounded off again to wave her mane in the springtime.

"What's the matter, Jean?" Mother said. "You've been so quiet lately. Is it only Grandmother?"

Jean could not tell her. She could not possibly let her mother know how rude and unfeeling she had been to Shirley Aimes.

"Do you think we'll have a house by September?" she asked in reply, stroking the kitten.

"Maybe," said Mother. "I'm taking a job on Monday, and then we'll see about the money."

"Where?"

"A restaurant near the dairy where Daddy works. I'll be waiting on tables. It won't be too hard because it's just mornings."

"Do you want to do it?" Jean asked, skeptical.

"I want a house," said Mother firmly. And from the way she said it, Jean knew that Mother's desperation matched her own.

They started walking again on the far side of the fence. The weeds came up to their waists, and the crickets and grasshoppers leaped at their feet.

Across the pasture, they could see Donald Harvie filling the horse trough with fresh water. He looked more like a cowboy than a farmer, Jean decided, with big boots and a wide-brimmed hat. She was about to ask Mother what she thought of him, when she saw Aunt Gwen come around the corner of the barn. And suddenly, before Jean could even think, Aunt Gwen was in his arms, and the wide-brimmed hat was shading them both. Donald Harvie's big hands came up and stroked Aunt Gwen's hair, and he kissed her right there by the horse trough.

"Mother!" Jean said, stopping.

Mother stood for a minute, half-turned toward the barn, and then she ducked her head down. "Oh, dear!" she said, smiling with surprise. "Jean, I don't think we should be watching."

But they watched anyway, huddled together in the weeds, far from the house and the barn.

"So now we know a secret," Mother said at last, afraid to move for fear Gwen might see her out by the plum trees. She watched while Aunt Gwen and Donald Harvie walked on into the barn with the water pails. "Well, perhaps it would be a good match. I'm glad that there's somebody else in her life besides . . ." She put her arm around Jean and looked suddenly serious. "Now listen, dear, not one word to anybody about this. When Aunt Gwen wants people to know, she'll tell them herself."

They reached the yard by coming in off the main road, and Jean put the kitten down. When she saw her aunt in the kitchen later, her cheeks rosy and her smile even brighter, Jean smiled back, liking her all the more because a man loved her. And then, she remembered what had happened at school, and wondered if she could ever be as lovable herself as Aunt Gwen.

Jean had never seen Donald Harvie up close. The nearest she had ever been to him was in church that one snowy morning with Aunt Gwen between them. Now she was even more anxious to find out what he was like.

She hadn't long to wait. On Saturday, she was balancing along a row of stones in the rock garden, when Grandmother came out the back door.

"Good land!" she exclaimed. "The man 'ud forget his right arm, he 'ud. Jean, lass, Donald Harvie's come an' gone an' left the jug o' buttermilk I put oot for him. Can ye hoist it across the field to his house yoursel'?"

Jean was not at all sure she could carry it, but she would have tied it to her back to get to see Donald Harvie's cottage.

"Sure," she said, lifting the jug in her arms.

" 'Tis the yellow bungalow on beyond the trees back o' the cornfield," Grandmother said, pointing to the north. "An' mind ye stay away from the river. Do ye hear me noo, Jean?"

Jean nodded and started off, her blue jeans making a whacking noise as her legs rubbed together. By the time she was out of sight behind the tractor shed, her arms ached and she set the jug down to rest.

The May sun was hot on her head as she started across the field. The newly plowed earth was soft under her feet. She wished she could roll the big jug, for it bore heavily down on her arms and bent her back.

There were trees all around Donald Harvie's yellow house, making a patch of shade on the ground, and Jean counted the steps until she reached it. There she set the jug down, too tired to walk the few steps more to the house.

"Hi, mole."

"Hi yourself." Jean didn't even bother to look up to know that Tommy Pepper was somewhere in the branches overhead.

There was a scraping noise as Tommy slid down beside her. "I saw you comin' a mile off," he said. "What'cha got in the jug? Whiskey?"

"No, silly. Buttermilk. If you saw me coming, why didn't you come out and help carry it?"

"Good for your muscles," Tommy grinned. He picked up the jug and Jean followed him into the bungalow.

The only rooms were a kitchen, a room that was part parlor, part bedroom, and a closed-in porch. There was a double bed in one corner of the parlor, a couch along the wall, a bookcase crammed full of old books, a lamp and chair, and a big dime-store map of the world.

Tommy set the jug on the kitchen counter. "You want a drink of it?"

Jean nodded, her mouth dry from the long hot walk. Tommy climbed up on the counter and took two large jelly glasses from the cupboard, slowly filling them with the thick yellow milk.

At that moment, the back door banged and the boy leaped off the counter. The big jug tipped on its side, and out came the milk down the side of the counter and onto the floor.

Donald Harvie entered the kitchen, his wet shirt clinging to his shoulders. He was taller than Aunt Gwen, taller than Jean's father even, but his body was so thin that his trousers seemed to hang loose from his belt, scarcely touching his legs. One hand, stained yellow with weeds, reached out and righted the jug.

"I spilt it," said Tommy.

"An' you'll be spillin' the rest if you're not careful." Donald Harvie did not smile at either Jean or Tommy, but his gentle voice was hardly the voice Jean expected from a man in western boots and hat. "The Grandmother sent it?" he asked Jean.

"Yes," Jean gulped, staring hard at the dirty face and trying to imagine Aunt Gwen kissing it. "She said you forgot it."

"It's a pretty big jug for a girl," Donald said, pouring some out in a third glass and drinking it down in big gulps.

Jean watched curiously. Nothing showed on the

tall man's face except weariness, the heat of the sun and the sting of the wind and the dust of the fields.

And then, without a word, Donald Harvie set his empty glass in the sink, and went back outside to hoe the small garden behind the house.

Jean watched him out the window. She felt she knew no more about him than she had before, and didn't want to. Would Father also be insensitive, gruff, and humorless after a few years as a farmer? Then she remembered the tall man kissing Aunt Gwen, holding her to him and tenderly touching her hair with one big hand. Maybe that's what women were for, up here in the land of Oshkosh. Maybe that's what was the matter with Grandmother, now that Grandfather was gone. She had no man to feed, no back to rub after a hard day's work in the fields, no big hands to reach down and help with the lifting and the hoeing and digging. *There was an old lady from Oshkosh. . . .*

Tommy Pepper was wiping out the inside of his glass with his finger and licking off the milk. "What you thinkin' on?"

"A silly rhyme, that's all," said Jean.

"Tell it to me."

"No. I won't."

"Tell me, and I'll let you in on a secret."

"Okay," said Jean, loving secrets. "There was an old lady from Oshkosh, who smothered us both with a washcloth."

Tommy Pepper waited. "Is that all?"

"Yes."

He wrinkled his nose disgustedly. "Listen. You want to know something really funny? You know what I'm going to do?" He took a mop from behind the stove and began swiping it lazily through the milk on the floor. "Soon as the carnival comes back, I'm gonna talk my Pa into leavin' and takin' me to Mobile, Alabama, where we come from. He always said he'd quit the carnival if I ast him, so I'm gonna ast. I ain't tellin' nobody we're leavin', 'cept Donald Harvie, maybe, and jus' before we take off, I'm gonna walk in your Grandma's house and I'm gonna tell her I seen a kelpie down by the river, just like that, and I think it were callin' my name. And the next day I'll be gone."

Jean had to laugh. "She'd never get over it."

Tommy Pepper chuckled loudly, showing a row of crooked teeth. "That's what I'm goin' to do. You wait and see. Soon as Pa gits here with the carnival."

Chapter 7

THE DOLLHOUSE was done. It was like no other house in the world. It had no glass in the windows, no chandelier in the dining room, no piano or refrigerator. It had, instead, a fireplace made of puffed wheat and glue, stair railings of raw spaghetti, and a real braided rug in the bedroom. There were live plants growing in window boxes outside the little kitchen, and a small mobile hanging from the ceiling at the top of the stairs. Bookshelves made of match boxes covered the wall on either side of the fireplace. The kitchen was bright with yellow enamel, and the dining room and den walls were papered with damask in one and burlap in the other. There was a screened porch on one side of the house, with real screen wire. There were beds and chairs made of alphabet blocks, covered with cotton and upholstered. There were acorn lamps, bottle cap bowls, thatched string chairs, button doorknobs, and velvet drapes from an old jacket.

"Aunt Gwen, it's like somebody really lived there!" Jean breathed.

"Of course," said Aunt Gwen, her huge face lit up. "We do. We were the ones who decorated the rooms and papered the walls and laid the floors and screened the porch. And it's ours to do with exactly as we please. What shall we do first?"

Jean laughed. "You know I'm too old to play with dollhouses."

"It doesn't matter," said Aunt Gwen. "What shall we do?"

"Have a Halloween party."

"In May?"

"Yes. There's someone I want to invite."

For a few days, the dream house was the center of attention. Mother added a few touches too, and there was a particular longing in her eyes that Jean understood. Grandmother, too, told the ladies at church, and often they would drive by of an afternoon to look at it over a cup of tea and Grandmother's raisin buns.

On Saturday evening, Jean called Shirley and invited her to come over. A car stopped in the drive, Shirley got out, and the car drove off. With her heart thumping painfully, Jean went across the lawn toward her.

"Is it done?" Shirley asked. "The dollhouse?"

"Yes. I wanted you to be the first to see it."

Still Jean could not look at her. She kept her eyes on the ground as they started toward the house.

"Why?"

The question was so direct that Jean stopped, embarrassed. Suddenly she said, "Because I wanted you to know I'm sorry about what I said that day."

Shirley broke a leaf off the lilac bush and stood rubbing it between her finger and thumb. "You didn't act like you were sorry."

Jean's voice quavered and she felt miserable. "I don't know why I did it. I really don't."

"Yes you do," said Shirley. "It was a way to get in with them."

Jean blinked. "But it was awful of me, and I'm really sorry. I felt terrible afterward."

"I know," said Shirley, as they went on towards the house. "I've done it too. But it never works out. I'm just waiting till the new school opens next fall, with thirty kids in each class. Then we'll see who fits in and who doesn't." She smiled good-naturedly. "In a big school there's room for all kinds. There are even nutty girls like me who have to practice piano every day."

"It's not really your piano lessons," Jean ventured.

"I know. It's everything. It's living in a big house and having all kinds of clothes. You'd think that would help, but it doesn't. We're city people living in the country, that's what, and I'm the citiest of them all."

They went upstairs to the bedroom where the dream house sat waiting. The shutters had been closed in Aunt Gwen's room, making it dark as the pitch on the roof. When Jean opened the door, Shirley drew in her breath and stared.

"Oh, Jean!" She crept inside and crouched down beside the dollhouse. "It's like a real fairy castle!"

A small birthday candle had been placed in each room of the dream house, and the flickering light cast tall shadows on the miniature walls and ceilings. A small black velvet cat which Aunt Gwen had purchased in the dime store sat before the fireplace. In the kitchen, a doll in black cape and high black hat leaned against the stove where a thimble pot was supposedly boiling, stirring the brew with a match stick. On the roof, a ghostly figure in a white handkerchief lifted its arms to the sky, and mystery seemed to lurk behind every shutter of the strange house, beneath the floorboards, and in the dark corners of the rooms above.

It was fun making things happen. Candles blew out, dark shadows passed in front of windows, and chairs disappeared. When Aunt Gwen came into the room later with sugared doughnuts and strawberry punch, the place was hopping with spooks.

"It's a beautiful house!" Shirley told Aunt Gwen. "How did you ever think of using burlap and buttons and bottle caps?"

Jean watched as Aunt Gwen's eyes sparkled in the candlelight, and her great jaws moved up and down on a doughnut. "It was fun," she smiled. "All my life I've wanted to make such a house, and when Jean came along, I found my excuse."

Jean named it Happening House. She could make the family inside rich enough to build a castle for Grandmother and keep her in it. She could make the girl in the house pretty, with hundreds of dresses. She could give Tommy Pepper a mother, and she could mix it all up with kelpies and hobgoblins which frightened Grandmother out of her wits. Happening House was whatever Jean wanted it to be, and she wasn't always sure just what that was.

"The carnival's come to town last evenin'," said big Angus at breakfast. "Settin' up on the lot west."

"I know," said Aunt Gwen. "I heard the donkeys braying this morning."

" 'Tis a cheap place to be," said Grandmother. "Decent folks do not go there."

"Can't we even go watch?" Brian asked.

"You can probably see all you need to from the top of the shed," Father said, a twinkle in his eye. "Mind I'm not tellin' you to crawl up there, of course."

Jean and Brian promptly went outside and climbed up on the tractor shed, straining to see. Jean wished the carnival were on the other side of the house so she could pass it going to school. Nevertheless, she and Brian could see quite a bit from the shed. They watched the big tents and the ferris wheel go up. Now and then they heard the foreign screech of an animal that shattered the peace of the barnyard and made the cows nervous.

" 'Twill be a miracle if it don't stop the cows' milk," Grandmother grumbled, limping off to the barn with the milk pails. "Such fool nonsense I never heard!"

At that moment Tommy Pepper came rushing around the silo. Before Grandmother had a chance to speak, he cried, "Miz McGinnis! Miz McGinnis! I saw it! I saw it!"

Jean stared. What in the world was he talking about?

Grandmother held out the milk pail as if to keep it between her and the wild-eyed boy. "Tommy Pepper! Wha' ails ye, boy? Wha' did ye see, child?"

"I saw it! Down by the river in the early mornin' fog! I saw it plain as the nose on my face, an' it says. . ."

"What? *What,* child?"

"A kelpie!" screeched Tommy, his eyes wide. "A kelpie big as an elephant, its legs stompin', and it says 'Tommy Pepper! Tommy Pepper!' in its faraway voice."

Grandmother clutched the milk pail to her breast, her eyes huge, but Tommy went on:

" 'Tommy Pepper! Tommy Pepper! Come to me! Come to me!' it says, just as plain."

Grandmother stretched out her hand, but Tommy edged backwards.

"Stay here, lad, stay here," Grandmother pleaded,

beginning to shake. "It's seen ye! It's come for ye!"

"I can't stay," Tommy gasped, backing around the corner of the tractor shed where Jean and Brian were standing. "I can't stay. The kelpie's callin' me. Oh, I got to go! I got to go."

Grandmother shrieked and rushed into the barn, banging the door fast behind her, moaning.

"Tommy!" Jean bent over and looked down at the elfin boy, who was rolling about on the ground in irrepressible glee. "Tommy!" she whispered. "Oh, you awful thing!"

But in a twinkling the boy was on his feet and streaking out through the walnut trees toward the carnival. "I'm goin' to see Pa!" he called back. "We're on our way!"

Grandmother was still moaning as the family drove to church later. Kelpies and carnivals and a full moon besides, she murmured. It was a forecast of things to come.

The news of the carnival had already reached the pastor. In his stiff white collar and black robe, he preached a sermon about the poor two-headed boy and three-legged girl which the carnival was exploiting, just as he had the year before and the year before that, and Jean wanted to go now more than ever.

" 'Tis a sin, tha' carnival," Grandmother declared as they rode back home again.

"Well, it brings them over for eggs and milk,"

Aunt Gwen said, looking in the direction of the tents as they pulled in the drive. "Last year we sold out all our eggs and milk when the carnival people were here."

The news traveled around the village. In righteous indignation with a touch of curiosity, the townspeople drove along the road slowly, straining their necks to catch a glimpse of the three-legged lady and the crocodile wrestler and the ape girl with hair all over her body, like the posters said. They scowled and shook their heads and clucked their tongues, just as they had each year before, and wondered what time it would open.

All afternoon the steady procession of cars moved slowly down the road past the farmhouse, on down past the carnival grounds where they slowed almost to a stop and then sped guiltily away. Grandmother sat on the sun porch as she always did on Sundays, dozing off now and then as the book in her lap dipped lower.

Aunt Gwen and Mother and Father went for a drive east of the village to see about a farm that was for sale, and Brian was digging a hole back in the grove. The house grew as still as the cornfields. Jean walked outside and over to the big rock at the top of the drive. She hated Sunday because of the forlorn quiet that settled down on the farm. Even the animals seemed to know it was Sunday. Now, with Tommy Pepper going to Mobile with his father, there wouldn't be any excitement at all.

She was still sitting there when a long white car pulled up the drive and stopped.

A heavy jowled face appeared, with two narrow eyes peeping out over the puffy cheeks. The heavy lips did all the moving when the man spoke, for he clenched a huge cigar between his teeth.

"Ga-ny-mil, girlie?" he said.

"What?" Jean asked.

A fat hand reached up and lifted the cigar momentarily.

"Got any milk for sale? Couple gallons, maybe?"

"I'll ask," Jean said, and ran quickly into the house.

"Grandmother," she said, shaking the old lady's arm. "There's a man outside who wants to buy milk."

Grandmother's head jerked up and she rubbed her eyes. "How much?" she grumbled. "I should go sellin' milk o' a Sunday?"

"Several gallons, I think."

That was different. Grandmother got up and lumbered outside.

"Murray Price," she whispered as she started across the lawn. "Might ha'e known. Who else 'ud come o' a Sunday?"

"Good morning, Grandmother! Another day, another season, eh?" The big man stretched out one hand but Grandmother ignored it.

"Mornin', Mr. Price. Didn't see ye in service this mornin', di' I?"

The big man's face took on an air of suffering. "My dear lady, it's been so long since I've seen the inside of a church, I'm ashamed to say. I am one of those unfortunate men whose work is seven days and seven nights, and my only rest is when it rains."

But Grandmother had no time for Murray's excuses. "Cost o' milk is up."

"Isn't it always, Grandmother? Ever since I first came this way, every summer another nickel?"

"More than a nickel this time," Grandmother said. "Seven cents the ha' gallon, an' I ought to make it eight o' a Sunday."

"Eight it is!" exclaimed the big man, pulling out his wallet. "Quality, Grandmother McGinnis! That's what I like about Wisconsin milk."

Grandmother went back to the huge refrigerator on the porch, and Jean stood by the lilac bush, watching.

Murray Price was not an attractive man. His pudgy hands looked almost like a child's, and his jacket barely reached around his huge middle, stretching at the button in front. His feet were small for so large a man, and his small eyes and ears and nose seemed lost in the huge expanse of fleshy face that shook and quivered with each puff of his black cigar.

Suddenly he wheeled around and said, "Five to one, girlie, five to one you're watchin' either my cigar or my money, right? Right, girlie?"

Jean jumped when he said it. "N . . . No," she

stammered. "I was looking at your tiny feet!" She was horribly embarrassed, but Murray Price laughed loudly, starting with a rumble and ending in a wheeze.

"My feet, eh? Got a fifty-cent cigar and a fifty-dollar bill in my wallet, and it's my feet what caught her eye!"

Grandmother came back out carrying a milk can and set it down heavily beside Murray. "Bring it back mornin's an' I'll fill it for ye, long as the cows don't stop milkin'. Sounds lik' a zoo in the mornin's, Mr. Price."

"That it does, that it does," Murray grinned, taking it as a compliment. "You really should come over, Grandmother." He lowered his voice to a whisper. "I've got the most fantastic animal you ever saw in your life, speakin' of zoos. Half bird, either a duck or a penguin, I don't know which, half dog, with the intelligence of a man and the feathers of a bird. It barks like a dog, jumps like a kangaroo, cries like a baby, brays like a donkey, and swims like a fish."

" 'Tis more sense ye should ha'e, Murray Price, goin' aboot pickin' up things wha' aren't meant to be seen," said Grandmother darkly. "Some day ye'll git ye a kelpie, an' 'twill be the last o' ye an' your carnival."

Murray Price laughed and got in the car, setting the milk can on the floor. Jean ran over.

"What's the name of it?" she asked eagerly.

"Of what, girlie?"

"The animal that barks and brays."

"Oh. It's a Duck-billed, Donkey-tailed, Bird-Dog, that's what it is," said Murray, and the car moved on down the drive with Murray's loud chuckle drifting back over the grass.

Halfway down the drive, the car stopped and Murray stuck his head out. "You've heard the news, Grandmother?" he called, his face suddenly serious. "A bad piece of luck."

"Eh?" said Grandmother, not quite hearing.

Murray Price started to call something else, then looked at Jean and stopped. "I'll be talkin' to you later. You'll be hearin' from Harvie, anyway." And the car rolled on with Grandmother staring after it, her hand shielding her eyes.

The next morning when Jean and her brother went to school, they wished they were going the other way. Far behind them, from the lot beyond the corn-field, came the bray of donkeys, the clank of hammers, and the rusty music of the carrousel.

Brian kicked at a rock, then ran after it and angrily kicked it again. "All we get to see are cows, cows, cows!"

Jean said nothing. That was exactly the way she felt too. Better one should go to a carnival and see a Duck-billed, Donkey-tailed, Bird-Dog, than go through life seeing only cows. She smiled to herself as she thought of Tommy Pepper rushing up to Grandmother with his fantastic story about seeing a kelpie, but quickly grew glum again. Tommy and his father were probably on their way to Alabama right now, and she hadn't even thought to tell him good-bye.

She felt as empty inside as the seat behind her, and all through the morning she thought how dull the farm would be without Tommy swinging down from the tractor shed, crawling up the side of the barn, or scrambling over the rock garden with Grandmother after him.

"Has anyone seen Tommy Pepper?" the teacher asked, but no one had.

At lunch time, everybody talked about the carnival. The ape girl, somebody said, was kept in a cage with a rope around her neck. The carrousel went so fast you almost fell off, others reported. The ferris wheel went so high that you could see over the tops of the trees.

The class that afternoon was restless. Mrs. Tulley took the children out in the meadows to look for the flowers pictured in their science books. Like spring lambs they romped and rolled in the grass, and Mrs. Tulley finally stopped trying to make herself heard, and sat down on the steps to make a chain out of the dandelion stems that were pressed in her lap.

At three o'clock, the teacher assembled the children in two straight lines and set them free. It was then that Jean discovered Brian and some of the other boys were missing.

Outside the playground, she looked quickly around. The small boy was nowhere in sight. Maybe, she reasoned, he had thought school was over and left early. But all the way home, as she thought more about it, she grew more sure of where Brian McGinnis had gone.

When she reached the drive, Grandmother came out to meet her.

"Where's the lad, Jean?" Grandmother called, the alarm rising in her voice.

"I don't know," Jean said. "We were lining up to walk home, and when I looked around for Brian, he had disappeared."

She could not have put it a worse way. Grandmother's hands flew up in the air, her mouth opened, and she rushed back into the house crying, "The kelpie's taken the lad! Rita! Gwendolyn! The kelpie's come for Brian!"

"Please, Grandmother," Jean begged. "He wasn't the only one. Some of the other boys are gone too, and so is Tommy Pepper."

The old lady shrieked even louder. Mother dropped the clothes she was sorting and came out into the kitchen. "What's the matter? Where's Brian?"

"I don't know," Jean told her. "Mrs. Tulley lined us up to go home and Brian wasn't there. I think he might. . ."

"What child, what?" gasped Grandmother.

"I think maybe he went to the carnival with some

of the other boys."

"Good heavens, Rita, a wee lad like tha' seein' wha' ain't fit to be seen by a grown man!" declared Grandmother. "Go fetch him back before he gets hypnotized by the ladies in the tents!"

Mother put a small scarf around her dark hair. "Come on, Jean," she said. "I'll need your help." And Jean followed eagerly, glad that she could go back to school the next day and tell the others she'd been.

Already the rusty clanking of the carrousel grated on the air, and there was a far-off blare of a loudspeaker which they couldn't understand. They could see the top of the ferris wheel revolving around above the trees, and now and then there was laughter or clapping.

"The Zoom!" Jean said as they rounded the bend. "See that big red and blue thing over there, Mother? Everybody at school is talking about it."

"We came to find Brian," Mother reminded. "Where do you think he would go first? The donkeys, maybe?"

They started across the carnival grounds toward the donkey rides, past the big brown tent where the crowd was standing.

"Ladies and gents, ladies and gents, never in your life if you live to be one-hundred will you see a show like the one in this tent. From the far corners of the globe I have captured the most exotic specimens of man and beast ever to be found in this hemisphere.

100

For the small sum of thirty-five cents, ladies and gentlemen, I invite you inside to see the fantastic, astonishing Duck-billed, Donkey-tailed, Bird-Dog, the rarest of all living animals. Come and see for yourself if Murray's carnival doesn't beat them all, bar none. If you are disappointed, all you need do, ladies and gentlemen, is turn right around and walk out the tent. But if you agree that the strange creature is beyond all you have ever seen, then for a small additional sum I invite you to stay for the most exotic of all human creatures, the ape girl. She has hair from her forehead to the soles of her feet. You'll see the three-legged lady, plus others I can't even describe. Step right up, ladies and gentlemen. That's the way, sir. Go right on in and get the best seat. Only thirty-five cents."

As the crowd began to move, Jean recognized the portly figure of Murray Price, cigar between his teeth, clutching a small microphone and wearing his straw hat with the red band around it.

At that moment he saw Jean. "Well, hello girls," he smiled. "So you've come to see my Duck-billed, Donkey-tailed, Bird-Dog after all, eh?"

"Not really," Jean said, while Mother stared in confusion. "We're looking for my little brother."

"Lookin' for her brother, the girl says. Well, won't be the first boy that's sneaked inside to see my famous Duck-billed, Donkey-tailed, Bird-Dog. You and your big sister go right in, and if you don't find him, come right out. But if you stay to see the show, I'll have to

101

charge you two tickets."

"Come on, Jean," said Mother, embarrassed. "We'll take one quick look, and if Brian's not there, we'll leave."

Inside, the crowd had gathered around a pit, lighted dimly at the bottom, and there walked the animal, just as Murray had said. It looked like a big dog, with a strange bill where its nose should have been, feathery protrusions on its sides like wings, and a long donkey's tail behind.

"It really is one, Mother," Jean cried, staring down at the animal. "Just like Murray said."

Mother didn't even look. She took Jean's hand and pulled her back outside.

"Not going already!" cried Murray, who was setting up the stage for the crocodile wrestler. "Not staying to see the three-legged lady I found in Australia?"

Mother pulled Jean on through the crowd, past the cotton candy palace and the ice cream stand, on toward the donkey rides at the edge of the field.

Sure enough, there by the rope where the line of children were waiting stood Brian, his eyes wide with wonder above his dirty red cheeks as he watched the donkeys moving around the ring with children on their backs. Mother had to shake him before he even knew she was there.

"Brian McGinnis, it's an angry father you'll have when he hears about this!" scolded Mother.

Brian stared at her sheepishly, but did not move.

102

He knew he would be punished, so did not see that it mattered if he stayed a bit longer.

"Need some help, Mrs. McGinnis?" said a low voice behind them, and Jean and her mother turned to see Donald Harvie, wearing his cowboy hat.

"Waitin' to have a talk with Mr. Price," Donald said, and then, smiling a little, looked at Brian. "Okay, cowboy. Either walk out of here like a man, or I'll have to carry you out, squealin' and kickin' front of all the other kids. You wouldn't like that, I'm thinkin'."

Brian looked up at the tall man and scowled. Slowly he shuffled back outside, yanking Grandfather's pipe from his pocket and sticking it defiantly in his mouth.

"Thank you," said Mother. "I didn't expect to meet anybody we knew."

"It's not exactly a social occasion," said Donald Harvie, speaking slowly. "You've heard the news, I reckon?"

"The news?"

"Tommy Pepper's father. Died a week before the carnival got here. The boy was told yesterday, and there's no comfortin' him."

Chapter

THERE WAS only one week of school remaining. Tommy Pepper did not come back at all, but the teacher promoted him anyway.

Jean walked to the front of the room in the white dotted swiss Shirley had given her, took her report card, and said good-bye to Mrs. Tulley. But she felt no great happiness as she usually did on the last day of school. Every time she thought of Tommy Pepper rushing barefoot over the fields, springing across the carnival lot and asking Murray Price where his Pa was, she felt like crying.

It wasn't that Donald Harvie wasn't good to Tommy. But he wasn't family, and now Tommy belonged to no one.

"It's no way for a boy to grow up," big Angus had said the night before, waxing his heavy boots on the

kitchen floor. "You've got to put your heart on someone and make your bed in a place you're special. Boy
don't belong to Donald Harvie no more'n the wind
does, and just as well, 'cause a boy needs motherin'."

Now, as Jean and Brian walked home from school,
hot in the June sun, something caught Jean's eye, and
she stopped. There in the clover field was a big
brown tent and a small truck.

"Another carnival!" Brian cried, breaking into
a run.

"Right in our field!" said Jean. "Do you suppose
Grandmother knows?"

They raced along the dusty shoulder of the road,
clutching their report cards.

"I'm telling Grandmother!" Brian cried, breaking
into a run.

"She must know," said Jean. "You can see where
they took down part of the fence to drive in."

Grandmother was shelling peas on the back steps.

"There's a carnival right out in our field!" Brian
yelled, falling onto the step beside her.

"A carnival!" Grandmother raised her eyes and
squinted toward the tent. "Tha's no carnival, lad.
Tha's Brother Henry Bean's revival meetin', an' he's
payin' rent by the week. Cannot see the harm in
lettin' oot land wha's only standin'. Maybe it'll take
folks away from the carnival an' put somethin' better
in their heads."

"What's a revival?" Jean asked.

" 'Tis a time for startin' a' over, Jeannie, puttin' away the bad an' takin' on the good. 'Tis a meetin' wi' songs an' prayers an' an invitation to do good. Tha's wha' it be."

"Can I go?"

"Not likely." Grandmother slowly hoisted herself to her feet and dropped the peas from her apron into the pan below. "You're a Presbyterian, and Brother Bean's no doot a Baptist or such. It'll only be confusin' to hear foreign preachin'."

"Oh, Grandmother!" Jean's cheeks blazed with anger. "Can't we ever do anything but sit in this old house and watch the cows?" Tears came to her eyes and she blinked to hold them back.

Grandmother looked at her silently, her face a mixture of surprise and reproach. But when she spoke, her voice was softer. "Is it so bad, then? Is it so bad wi' the cows an' chickens, the plantin' an' hayin'?"

Jean could not answer. What could she possibly say except yes, and she didn't trust herself to say it politely.

"Ye'll not be goin' to the meetin's, but if your faither says there's no harm, ye can go to the tent between times. If Brother Bean's willin' to ha'e ye, o' course. Come now, lass, an' wash your face, an' we'll ha'e some ice cream an' buns."

"I'm not hungry," said Jean. She threw her books down on the grass and walked back to the grove behind the house to escape the heat. Even the kittens grew lethargic in the heat. Back in Logan, the last day of school would have caused a celebration. All the kids would be out on the sidewalk, skating up and down the hill or bicycling around the block. But not here. Not among the cows and the clover, the chickens and pigs, the silent waving meadows and the dust of the road.

Brian followed, surprised at the way she had spoken to Grandmother.

"You know what I saw last night, Jean?" he asked. "Right there where that rock is?"

"What?"

"A rat. A rat as big as a billy goat."

That made it all the worse. It wasn't enough that there was the squeaking and scratching and sliding of mice in the ceiling at night above the beds in Aunt Gwen's room. But there were rats beneath the barn and the tractor shed, and who knew what else?

"Come on, Jean," said Brian. "Let's go have some ice cream."

"I said I don't want any," Jean snapped. "Go get some yourself and leave me alone."

Brian frowned at her and went back to the house. Jean sat down in the shade of the grove, breathing in the dank moldy odor of the underbrush. She knew she'd been rude, but she didn't care. The undercurrent of anger boiled inside her, and she could think of nothing pleasant to say to anybody. It wasn't only Grandmother. She was angry at herself, for she knew that it wasn't just enough food, enough clothes and a dollhouse that she wanted. She wanted excitement and adventure. All her life there would be something she wanted that she didn't have.

Across the wide cornfield she could see Donald Harvie's house. As she watched, she saw Tommy Pepper come out and sit down on a bench. Jean could tell that he, too, felt the heat, the boredom, and besides all that, the sadness nobody else could feel except him.

Without thinking twice, she jumped up and started across the hot field.

Tommy watched her come. His eyes seemed darker than they had before, and he was not smiling.

"I saw you out in the yard, so I came over," Jean said.

Tommy did not answer.

Jean sat down. "What are you going to do this summer, Tommy? I heard about your father. I'm awfully sorry."

Tommy took a deep breath. "I'm goin' with the carnival when it moves on. Takin' Pa's place."

"Oh."

Jean was quiet when she heard it. She had hoped he'd say that Donald Harvie had asked him to stay on. "When is the carnival leaving?" she asked finally.

Tommy shrugged. "Couple weeks, I suppose."

"Maybe you'll go to a city next. Wouldn't you like that?"

"Cities are okay."

"Don't you like them better than country?"

"Depends. Home was always where Pa was. Wherever we was, I liked it fine."

Jean tried hard to think of something that would cheer him up. "You know, Grandmother still believes you saw a kelpie the other day."

A smile played on Tommy's lips, then disappeared. "It didn't work out like I wanted."

Jean put her arms around her knees. "Daddy said if Grandmother didn't have her superstitions she'd go crazy, just facing the cows every day. She even sings to them. Did you know that?"

Tommy stood up, tired of talking about Grandmother. "I'm hot. I'm going back and wade in the river. Come on."

"Grandmother would have a fit."

"Your Pa wouldn't care, would he?"

"I don't think so."

"Then come on."

Jean followed him through the trees to the river in her best white dress.

It was cool by the river. Tommy Pepper led the way where the bank sloped down to the muddy water. As he stepped barefoot into the slow-moving current, the thick black mud oozed up between his toes and gave him an obvious sense of delight.

"Ick!" said Jean, backing up. "It looks awful."

"Close your eyes, then," Tommy told her.

Jean resolutely waded in, gritting her teeth as her feet sank heavily in the soft stuff underneath.

"Ugh!" she whispered. "What if there are worms?"

"Worms, crabs, kelpies, all sorts of things," Tommy said, his laugh beginning to sound like it used to.

"Tommy," Jean said suddenly, following along behind him. "What do you do if you want something you can't have?"

"Git it if I can," said Tommy. "Settle for somethin' else, or forgit about it."

"I don't forget very easily," said Jean. "When I want something I keep thinking about it."

"Guess that's how I feel about Pa," said Tommy.

"Did you ever want anything else that you couldn't have?"

"Yep. A pig."

"A pig!"

Tommy grinned. "A baby pig to raise myself. Can't raise a pig in a circus truck, though."

"Why would you want a pig?" Jean asked incredulously.

"One time me and Pa stopped at a county fair, down in Missouri, I think it was. And I saw a boy with a great big hog, and he's got hisself a blue ribbon for it. And he's tellin' how he took the pig when it was young, and fed it and brushed it hisself, and got a heap of money for it. Only I think maybe I wouldn't sell mine. I'd just sort of keep it around to look at and know it was mine and think about how little it was onct." He glanced at Jean. "What do you want?"

Jean laughed a little. "Excitement, I guess."

"Wait till Tuesday. There'll be some excitement then."

"What's happening? Where?"

"A rat killing. In your barn. Donald said so."

"They're going to kill a rat?"

"A hundred or so. All they can find. Goin' to smoke 'em out and shoot 'em."

What a horrible thing, Jean thought. What a ghastly thing to do right in somebody's yard!

They oozed along through the mud, and Jean began to enjoy the coolness of the water on her legs, listening to the faint gurgle as the water rippled over the rocks in the middle.

Suddenly she stopped, clutching at Tommy's shirt. "Tommy! Look ahead! That horse!"

Far down the river, a gray horse, as light as mist, stood erect in the water, its head turned toward them, its tail flicking back and forth as if it were ready to run.

"So it's a horse," said Tommy. "What of it?"

"How do you know it is?"

"Well, it sure ain't a cow. Watch." Tommy Pepper gave a loud whistle and the horse took a step forward, its body tense.

"Oh, Tommy, *don't!*" Jean cried. "Grandmother says. . ."

"Helloooooooooo."

Jean covered her mouth in terror as the call came echoing down over the water, and then she saw a man emerge from the trees on the bank.

"See! It's only a man watering his horse," said Tommy. "Let's go see who he is."

Ashamed, Jean splashed through the water beside Tommy. The man sat down again and rested his arms on his knees. His blond hair was thinning and his eyes had a kind of hollow, ethereal look that spoke of many things. He had on a pair of black trousers and a plain white shirt which was open at the collar. He smiled as Jean and Tommy came up the bank.

"You gave me a scare," he said. "When you whistled, I thought I might lose my horse, and since she's really not mine, I'd have no right to lose her, you know."

"Whose is she, then?" asked Tommy.

"Farmer who lives down the road. My truck broke down, so he loaned me his horse while I'm here." He extended his hand. "Bean's the name. Brother Bean. I'm the preacher who's holding the revival. You've seen the tent, maybe?"

"Oh, yes," said Jean. "Grandmother said I could visit you if I didn't go to the meeting."

"If you didn't go to meeting, eh?" The man smiled to himself and scratched his knee. "And what about the carnival tents down the road the other way?"

"Oh, I'm not allowed there either," Jean said hastily.

"I see. What's your name?"

"Jean McGinnis. And this is Tommy Pepper."

"How do you do, Tommy?" The man leaned back against a tree. "Why don't you sit down and talk while the horse is drinking? It's nice to see someone around besides cattle. Cattle don't come to meeting either."

Tommy sat down and cleaned the mud out from between his toes with a stick. "Jean thought you was a kelpie," he said. "The horse, I mean."

Jean flushed.

"A kelpie?" asked Brother Bean. "What's that?"

Tommy laughed. "Ask the old grandmother. She's the only one what's seen 'em."

"It's sort of a ghost," Jean explained. "But it looks like a horse. And when it sees you, it calls your name, you leap on its back, and it will take you down under the water to the other world."

Brother Bean sat looking at Jean as though he did not understand a word she was saying. Then slowly, he began to shake his head. "In this day and age!" he said. "In this day and age, and the Grandmother is afraid of the meeting, yet!"

No one quite knew what to say after that. Jean tried to think of something solemn and serious to talk about to a preacher. At last she said, "Tommy Pepper's father died last week. And it's all the family Tommy has."

Brother Bean turned to Tommy. "No other relatives at all? What will you do?"

"I'll eat," Tommy said, a false bravado in his voice. "I'm goin' back to the carnival where Pa worked. They'll take me on."

"Your father was a carnival man?"

"All his life," said Tommy. "Weren't hardly a state we ain't been in, from Texas to Maine."

For a while the preacher did not say a word. He picked up a blade of grass and rolled it back and forth between the palms of his hands. "Though it's hard to see," he said finally, "there might have been a reason for it."

"For Tommy's father dying?" Jean asked. "Of course there was. He was sick. Murray Price said so."

Brother Bean shook his head. "Only one thing can destroy the life of a man, and that's sin."

Tommy Pepper jerked his head. "What do you know about my pa and sinnin'? Reckon I knowed him better'n you."

The gaunt man was not disturbed. "If a man could live without sin, he could live forever. But so far, no one has been able to do it."

Jean looked at him curiously. "Are you a Baptist?"

"No, child. My religion goes by no name. It's part of me, that's all."

"Well, it sounds pretty gloomy."

114

"Not at all. There's always hope. If every man truly, truly repented of his deeds, he would never die. But there's always something we do that we ought not that makes us say, 'He deserved it,' or 'I couldn't help it,' and so all of us go to the grave with some little sin that pride kept us from repenting."

What a beautiful thought, Jean was thinking. If all the people of the world repented of their sins, they would all live forever.

"It's nuts, you know." Tommy Pepper broke the silence with a rude laugh. "If people went on living, there wouldn't even be room to sit down and take your shoes off. Everybody's got to die some time." He stood up and skipped a stone out over the water, startling the horse. Jean got up too.

"I've got to go back, Tommy. If Grandmother knew I was here she'd be frantic."

"Tell her where you was, then," said Tommy. "Tell her you didn't see no kelpie, just a crazy man what's going to live forever."

Brother Bean smiled and waded out to get the horse. "Not me either, boy. I've got sins as black as anybody's, and a pride just as fierce. No, the blind leads the blind, I'm afraid."

As he brought the horse up the bank, he said. "Would you like a ride back to the farmhouse?"

"Could I?" asked Jean. "You come too, Tommy."

Brother Bean made a stirrup of his hands, and Jean climbed on first, then Tommy. The preacher swung himself up behind them. When they reached the field, the horse went trotting down between the rows of corn, the long green leaves brushing Jean's legs, until at last they came to the yard beside the house.

Jean and Tommy slid off and watched as the preacher went on.

"Come tonight if it's only to sing," he called, and then he was out of sight behind the barn.

Chapter **9**

IT WAS A solemn supper and, as the evening wore on, things got worse. Mother sat by the window on the sun porch, mending Brian's trousers. Big Angus sat on the other side of the room, smoking his pipe and listening to the news on the radio. Every so often he looked at Grandmother, then at Mother, and went on puffing. Aunt Gwen was out milking the cows, and Brian was with her. Jean could hear his laughter, which made an eerie contrast to the silence in the house.

"Well, out with it," said Father at last, snapping off the radio. He took the pipe from his mouth and tapped it against the ash tray, looking at Grandmother all the while. "All you've told me is that Jean was disobeyin'. What's the lass done?"

Grandmother pursed her lips and jerkily flipped

the pages of her magazine. "A' she shouldn't," she replied. "A' I've ever tol' her not."

"That's not tellin' much," said Father. "I can't be punishin' her for everything. What happened then, after she got home from school?"

"Offered her some ice cream, I di', but she 'ud ha'e none o' it. Off she goes through the trees in a huff. An' then she was gone. It was as if a kelpie had come into the yard an' taken her off."

Jean sat sullenly in a chair by the doorway, scowling down at her dirty bare feet. For heaven's sake, didn't Grandmother ever think of anything else?

"I searched the farm over, the sun beatin' doon an' supper waitin'. An' just as I come back to the house to put the bread in, I hear a horse trottin' up, an' I look oot to see Jean on its back, an' its lik' to tak' my heart!"

"Jean came home on a horse?" asked Father, turning to his daughter. "Whose horse was it, lass?"

"The preacher's," answered Grandmother, without giving her time to speak. "There she be, perched up there wi' the preacher himsel' an' Tommy Pepper to boot. She's been to the river, she tells me, in her Sunday dress, an' wha's more, she brings tha' boy right in the kitchen askin' for a drink. The bread fell, my ankles swelled, the sky clouded up, an' who knows wha' will happen next?"

Big Angus looked at Jean and slowly lit his pipe. "I've no objection to her goin' to the river, Mother.

Donald Harvie says it's a slow one, and not over four feet most places."

Grandmother stopped fidgeting with the magazine. "She's your daughter, Angus. If ye care no more'n tha'."

"Nonsense, Mother. There are worries enough without addin' the kelpies."

Mother cleared her throat. "Jean, you should have told Grandmother where you were going. I can imagine how worried she must have been."

But Grandmother McGinnis ignored it. "She's your daughter, Angus," she repeated, "Ridin' horseback wi' the preacher an' goin' to the river, I've no say. But when it comes to bringin' tha' boy in my kitchen, I won't ha'e it!"

"I've something to say on that."

The voice came from the doorway of the sun porch. Jean looked up to see Aunt Gwen standing there, her face serious and the twinkle gone from her eye.

"I say the lad can go where he pleases, Mother. To turn a boy out for no reason is bad enough, but to turn out a boy with no family is sin itself."

The silence that followed was so deep that Jean was terrified. Grandmother rose, and she and Gwen stood facing each other, their arms at their sides, eyes unblinking. Then, without a word, Grandmother moved past Aunt Gwen, across the dining room, and into the back bedroom, shutting the door.

But Jean was not prepared for what happened

next. Aunt Gwen sat down on the couch, put her face in her hands and began to sob.

Angus leaned forward. "It had to come, Gwen. You did right."

But Aunt Gwen did not answer.

"Go outdoors now where it's cool," Mother said to Jean. "We've things to talk about."

Jean got up quickly and went out across the wet grass. "All because of me," she told herself, hurting inside because of Aunt Gwen's hurt, and she closed her eyes tightly.

On the other side of the fence, separating the cow pasture from the clover, two rows of cars were parked. Lights burned inside the tent, and a sign said simply, "Revival—8 o'clock."

Jean crawled over the fence and waded through the tall grass to the tent, where June bugs buzzed around the light, and the smell of sawdust, of tired men and women, of canvas chairs, and mildewed hymnals mingled with the fresh smell of damp clover.

There was a squeaking of chairs from inside as a prayer ended, and the men and women sat back down. There were leathery, red-necked farmers, stiff in white shirts and once-a-week neckties, and farm women in starched house dresses, with a rose pinned to their bosoms or a brooch on their shoulders.

A phonograph started to play, slowly at first, but picking up speed as the machine warmed up, and the wavering voices of the congregation joined the strong, clear voice of Brother Bean:

I'm redeemed, praise the Lord!

I'm redeemed by the blood of the Lamb.

I am saved from all sin, and I'm walking in the light,

I'm redeemed by the blood of the Lamb.

Jean sat down beside one of the cars, the clover tickling her legs and the crickets leaping across her lap. Were they really saved from sin? Would the woman in the faded print dress and the bald man with suspenders go on living forever? Was it true that Brother Bean could go about the country redeeming others but could not save himself?

She crept forward on her knees so she could see him better. He looked very different tonight as he stood in front of the people, his face radiant and his eyes misty. And as his wonderful voice came rolling out the door of the tent, Jean thought that if anybody in the whole world should live forever, it was Brother Bean.

When the last verse had ended, the people stopped singing, but the music went on. And now Brother Bean was talking very softly, inviting the men and women to come to the altar and repent of their sins, to make their souls as clean as the rain. Then they would know the glories of living forever, from this day forward.

He stopped a moment and then said it all over

again. This time he spoke even softer and more earnestly than before. Someone in the back row got up and started down the aisle.

As the music went on, Jean felt her eyes smarting with tears, and she made no effort to keep them back. There she was, crying in the wet clover just as Aunt Gwen was crying back there on the sun porch. She longed to stand up and walk down that aisle herself, to kneel down beside that wonderful man and ask repentence of everything she had ever done and ever would do.

At that moment her eye caught something on top of the tent, and she rocked back on her heels. There sat Tommy Pepper with a smile as wide as a man's hand.

Jean gasped. How could he? How *could* he? It ruined everything, and he did not even care.

Tommy motioned to something in his lap and, as Jean watched, he picked up a handful of green cherries and rolled them down the tightly stretched canvas where they hit the ground with soft thumping noises.

"Tommy!" Jean whispered, as the people in the back row raised their heads and looked toward the roof.

> *Just as I am, without one plea,*
> *Thou Lamb of God, who died for me. . . .*

Another song came softly from the phonograph. Up in front, Brother Bean stood with eyes closed, hands uplifted, and more people rose from their seats and started down the sawdust aisle, dabbing at their eyes as they came.

With a wild rattling, another handful of stone-hard cherries came rolling down the sloping tent, and the people looked around.

Jean sprang to her feet. She rushed back across the field, flung herself over the fence, and buried her face in the long grass of the cow pasture. Brother Bean was true and good and wonderful, and Tommy Pepper was wicked. She hated everything that had happened since she had come, and wished she were anywhere in the world but the great, wide countryside around Oshkosh.

It was cooler on Tuesday. The breeze seemed to help Grandmother's disposition, for she went out of her way to do little things for Jean and Brian, and even smiled occasionally at Mother. But she did not smile at Gwen. There was a coolness now between them that was hard to cover up.

At breakfast Grandmother said, "The neighbor men are comin' by this afternoon for the barn cleanin'. Might want to see if ye can git home early, Angus, an' help oot."

"I'll come home at three," said Jean's father. "Got any shells for the gun, Mother?"

"What do you need shells for to clean a barn?" Brian asked.

"Goin' to clean it of rats," said his father. He

turned to Grandmother and waited.

"A couple boxes on the shelf," said Grandmother. She grunted, her eyes avoiding Gwen's. " 'Course, Donald Harvie'll come wi' an empty barrel hopin' we'll supply him."

Aunt Gwen said nothing.

"Why not?" said Father. "Aren't his rats. I'll pick up another box or two for good measure."

It was the rat killing, just as Tommy had said. Jean knew she was going to watch, in spite of her horror. There was something thrilling in the gruesomeness that appalled her, and she found she could hardly talk about it. But finally it was afternoon, and a car drove up with six burly men. Brian squealed with excitement, and Jean knew it was time.

Donald Harvie was working around the barn, chasing all the pigs out and herding the colt to the pasture. Tommy Pepper was there too, chasing the hens and turkeys from the hay mow and hanging around the men outside. Father came home early as he had promised and instructed Jean and Brian to stay on the back porch.

Jean watched Tommy Pepper climb on the roof of the tractor shed, and turned away in disgust. How he could possibly have done what he did at the revival was beyond her. Now he was dancing around on top of the shed as though he were watching a circus. Even Grandmother put on a fresh apron and went out to sit in the rock garden. Aunt Gwen and Mother, how-

124

ever, remained in the kitchen, frying chicken for supper.

Big Angus took the gun off the wall, loaded it, and went outside. Donald Harvie was shoveling leaves and muck from a pit under one end of the barn. He threw in some wood and paper, lit them, and with a big slab of tin, covered the fire in such a way that the smoke poured right under the barn.

Jean stood at the screen door, a feeling of dread spreading through her. She loathed rats. Whenever she saw one near the silo, she was gripped with terror. But great big men with guns, killing them, was all too horrible.

Tommy saw Jean in the doorway. "Just watch!" he yelled. "Some'll be bigger'n cats, bigger'n jack rabbits, even."

"My daddy'll get 'em all," Brian shouted back. "He'll get more'n anybody."

Mother came out on the porch and stood behind Jean, wiping her hands slowly on the dish towel, her eyes intent on the men. The smoke from the fire grew blacker and the men took their places, one at each corner of the barn. Big Angus stood between the house and the rock garden with his gun ready, watching. A faint wisp of smoke began to curl out from under the barn. The men raised their shotguns.

Suddenly it came. A small, dark object, ran swiftly out from under one corner of the barn, hugging the ground with its belly, its tail flat against the earth.

A yell went up from the men and a gun cracked. The rat ran another two feet and fell on its side.

The smoke grew blacker now and began rolling out from all sides of the barn, as if the great gray building itself were on fire. Another gun fired, and then two more from behind the barn.

Something leaped down from a window of the barn and headed for the house.

"Get it, Angus, lad!" screamed Grandmother, and Father's gun exploded just as Jean shrieked.

"Did ya see that one?" Tommy Pepper cried. "As big as a. . ."

He did not finish, for the creature that lay on the path to the house was not a rat at all, but one of Patches' kittens.

Jean screamed again, and started to fling open the door, but Mother held her back.

"A kitten!" Jean cried. "Oh, Mother, he shot a kitten! Daddy shot it!"

"Angus." Jean had never heard her mother say it quite like that. The cold, disbelieving tone seemed to stretch the distance between her parents into miles.

Big Angus stood in the yard, staring helplessly at the kitten there on the path. "Couldn't help it, Rita," he said. "Thought we got 'em all out. I'm sorry, lass."

But there was no time for apologies. Suddenly rats were coming from all directions, crawling up from under the barn, and leaping from windows. Father loaded his gun again and fired.

126

Jean turned quickly and ran back through the kitchen, her face white. For a moment her eyes met Aunt Gwen's.

"It couldn't be helped, Jean," said Aunt Gwen from the window where she'd been watching. "Patches' kittens lead reckless lives, and if it wasn't the gun, it would be the river or the horse trough or rat poison or something. They don't live forever."

Jean gave her aunt a bewildered stare. How could she talk like that? It was the smallest kitten, with white paws like Patches, and Father had shot it down like a barnyard rat!

Aunt Gwen's face was tense with the weariness of the farm, and she did not smile. "That's the way it is on a farm, Jean. You have to learn country ways."

Jean ran quickly upstairs to the bedroom, gulping frantically as the tears seemed to back up and cascade down her throat. Aunt Gwen, too? Couldn't anybody in this house understand about feelings and people and wanting everything alive to go on living? And suddenly, in great revulsion, she knew she hated the farm. She hated the monotony, the poverty, the silences and the crudeness, and she wondered if the McGinnis family would ever be happy again. She did not think it would.

It was a hard time for Jean. It was worse now that school was out. Now there was no where else to go, and the boredom, the nothingness of the barn and the cows and the red hot sun on the dusty fields grew stronger with each passing day. Every time she looked at Donald Harvie, especially at his dirty hands and sweat-soaked shirt, and thought of Aunt Gwen loving him, she was filled with disgust. She made no effort to talk when she saw him about.

It was affecting Mother too. She did not smile as often as she had back in Logan, and there was little to smile about then. Jean overheard her talking to Father one morning as they left for work.

"I can't help it, Angus," she was saying. "It's like I wasn't even married. I'm just another girl for Grandmother to order around. I want a place of our own!"

"And so do I!" said Father impatiently. "Hasn't anything turned up, at least nothin' we can pay. It's the way you slip in and out that turns me. You're always movin', never stoppin' to pass the time of day with her."

"You would get out too if she was always criticizing you," Mother retorted. "And she doesn't have to say a word. I can see it in her eyes."

"You're readin' things that aren't there," Father said moodily, climbing in the car and slamming the door. He waited until Mother got in the other side, then started the motor. "Long's it has to be this way, might as well make the best of it. Won't hurt you none to smile or to ask of her health now and then."

Mother replied with a toss of her dark head, and the car moved on. Jean sat motionless by the house.

They hadn't quarreled so much in Logan. No matter what went wrong, they had still smiled at each other. But not now. The farm did away with smiling.

Across the pasture she could see Brother Bean moving about outside his tent. She got up and headed out past the barn.

As she was climbing the fence by the plum trees, she realized the preacher wasn't alone. Murray Price's long white car was parked beside the small truck, and the two men were sitting by the tent, eating hamburgers from a paper sack.

"Ah! Company for breakfast!" Murray said, holding the bag out toward Jean. "Help yourself, girlie."

"I just ate," said Jean.

"Well, sit down and watch two starving men, then," said Brother Bean, smiling at her with his misty eyes.

Jean sat down on the grass.

"Not looking for a job, are you?" Murray asked. "My three-legged girl just ran off to Nebraska with some sailor."

"How could I help?" said Jean. "I've only got two legs."

Murray Price chuckled, his chest moving rapidly in and out. "So did Dottie, so did Dottie," he wheezed.

"So that's it!" said Jean. "Mother said it was a trick."

Murray went on chuckling, but Brother Bean showed neither amusement nor reproach. He slowly took another bite of hamburger and looked at the cornfields which stretched all the way to the carnival. "I don't see how you figure it, Murray," he said after a time. "A fraud is a fraud."

"Why, Brother Bean! Not so! Not so!" Murray gave a look of shocked innocence. "A cheat for the sake of cheating is one thing but a fraud for the purpose of charity, quite another."

"How can you call it charity?"

"It's the truth, Brother." Murray Price continued to eat rapidly, turning the sandwich around and around in his hands as he spoke, examining it from all angles. "It's like this. I take the rejected, the nobodies, and I give 'em a purpose. The ape girl was given me by her parents when she was fifteen years old. Had her locked in the house all day so she wouldn't get out and scare anybody, poor thing. Like a dog, she was, with hair all over her neck and her arms, and hangin' an inch off each elbow. So I put her in my carnival, and now she's a star."

"But she's real," said the preacher. "How about the three-legged girl? How do you explain that one?"

"Ah!" Murray continued turning his sandwich around, taking a bite off each corner until there was nothing left. Then he reached into the sack for another, which he unwrapped without missing a word. "Dottie was a wild bird, that I can tell you. She came to the carnival one night with a guy from Michigan, and he left her there by the ferris wheel. Wouldn't even take her home. I could see she'd been around plenty, and when I asked her about it, turns out she'd left home a year before, had her share of trouble, and lookin' like she might be in for some more.

"'Dottie,' I says, 'You need a job. You need regular work and meals you can count on.' And so I told her about the three-legged lady, and I tell you, sir, she was the best I ever had. Not only that, but she was a sweet-tempered young girl with a sense of humor, and there wasn't a soul in the world that didn't like her."

"So now she's off to Nebraska with a sailor," said Brother Bean.

Murray sighed. "So she is. That's the way it goes. But for two months, at least, I gave her a living, and I can wager it was a cleaner slice of life than what she'd ever cut herself before."

"What about the people who came expecting to see bona fide attractions?" asked the preacher. "What right have you to cheat them?"

Murray paused a moment with his sandwich in his hand and his big mouth strangely taut. When his lips began to chew again, he said, "Ah, brother, you shock me. You really do. Do you think that if the village folks didn't come to my sideshows, the silver would be clinking in your offering plate instead? No, Brother Bean, money that would have gone for drinkin' and gamblin' and other kinds of sin, that's the money I get. Every Friday that I got a carnival going in a neighborhood, it's a dozen more souls I've kept out of the saloon and pool halls, and instead of goin' for liquor, the dollars go to pay the livin' expenses of poor freaks that haven't a chance on the outside."

It was certainly confusing, Jean decided, listening to each man talk. Both of them seemed to make sense.

"Brother Bean," she said quickly, noting the lull in the conversation, "I just wanted to say I'm sorry about what Tommy Pepper did the other night. It was awful of him."

Murray looked up. "What's the boy done now?"

"He was sitting on the tent while the meeting was going on," Jean explained, "and rolling green cherries down the canvas and making a terrible noise." She looked at the preacher. "I was afraid you would think it was me."

"I know," said Brother Bean. "I saw you get up and run home. But you missed the best part."

"What happened?"

Brother Bean turned and pointed to the roof of the tent. There, right where Tommy had been sitting, was a huge rip in the canvas.

Jean gasped. "Did he fall?"

"Yes. He landed right beside me. Lucky he wasn't hurt, but I doubt he'll try it again. His face looked like a wild strawberry, and he streaked out the door like a wet cat."

Jean laughed. If only she'd seen it! What a perfect thing to happen to a boy who insisted on having his feet in the air!

132

Murray Price took out his wallet. "He's my charge, I guess, and I mean to pay his way, mistakes and all."

"No, I want nothing," the preacher said. "It was a boyish prank. I'll fix the canvas myself. Besides, I'm already indebted to you for this meal and for having my truck repaired."

Murray shrugged. "Man cannot go on spirit alone. You've got to have a little bread in your stomach if you expect to preach a good sermon."

Brother Bean smiled a little. "What do you think would make a good sermon, Murray?"

The big man turned around. "Me," he said. "The carnival." He leaned forward and put one pudgy hand on the preacher's arm. "I'm serious, Brother. Tell 'em all the reasons they shouldn't come to my den of iniquity. It'd be a great talk."

"I was planning to do just that," said Brother Bean, a puzzled smile on his face. "But I doubt we'd be friends again."

"Friends forever," said Murray, shaking his hand. "I promise you, Brother Bean, whatever you might say against me and my sideshows, I welcome as an honest opinion from an upright man."

"I don't understand you, Murray," said the preacher.

"Don't try," said Murray, getting into his car. "Don't try. Good afternoon, girlie, and good preaching, Brother!"

Chapter *10*

JEAN WENT to town with her father on Friday night. "Town" was a little shopping center on the outskirts of Oshkosh, and on Friday evenings everybody from the farm community for miles around drove there to buy or to stand outside the five and ten and talk for an hour or so.

They parked outside the laundromat and walked up to the corner to buy feed for the chickens.

"Want to pick out the feed sack, lass?" asked Father as he paid the lady.

"That one over there," said Jean, choosing a cloth bag with small green flowers on it. "Grandmother's saving them for sun porch curtains."

They took the lawn mower to the hardware store to be sharpened, and big Angus gave his daughter a dime.

134

"I'm getting a haircut over at Earl's. Have yourself an ice while you're waitin'."

Jean bought a raspberry ice and walked up and down the sidewalk, swirling it around on her warm tongue. As she passed the gas station, she saw Donald Harvie having his car washed.

She stared. She had gotten so used to the thick coat of dust and grime on his car that she had no idea it was blue underneath. And if she had ever thought of seeing it clean, she would have imagined Donald himself doing the scrubbing.

But there he was, dressed in his Sunday suit, with his shoes shined and his hair slicked down. He was holding a neat gray dress hat with a black band.

"Think I'll have to give 'er another go-round, Mr. Harvie," the attendant was saying. "Can't get a five-year's accumulation off in one scrubbin'."

"You'd charge me double?" asked Donald.

"Noooo. Guess not. Say half again as much would be fair. Dollar fifty?"

"Okay. I want it done good."

Jean stood off to one side, watching. She had never seen Donald Harvie so dressed up, not even at church. She stared at his clean-shaven face and the hands which had been relentlessly scrubbed of grease and stains, so that even the nails looked strong and white. She thought of saying something to him, but the way he kept glancing at his watch made her feel that he might not have time to talk. She backed away and went to meet Father, thoughtfully sipping the ice.

Big Angus was still in the barbershop, however, so Jean sat down on the bumper of his car and waited. Three women came out of the laundromat, pausing to finish their conversation.

"He's good, I tell you," the woman in the brown slacks said to the others. "Jim and I went to hear him last night, and he really laid it on about the carnival. Why, the things that Murray Price gets away with, there ought to be a law!" She laughed uneasily. "Jim says now we ought to go back to the carny again and see if it's as bad as the preacher says."

The other women smiled.

"I'm going out to service Sunday, so I'd better go to the carnival tomorrow. Then I'll know what the brother's talking about," one of them said.

"That three-legged girl, she sure looked real enough," the third woman said. "All a hoax, says Brother Bean. I got to go back and prove it to myself."

The first woman transferred her bundle to her other arm. "Well, it's good old-fashioned fire 'n brimstone preachin', that's sure. Ain't too many of them kind around no more. Thought I ought to take the boys once and let 'em hear too."

Then he was doing it, Jean thought. Brother Bean was preaching out against the carnival just as Murray had asked him to do. And it sounded as though the more people came to hear him preach, the more they went to the carnival to see what he was talking about.

The moon that night was as round and yellow as a pumpkin, and Jean sat at the window looking down at the barn and the fields and the faraway light in Donald Harvie's cottage.

"Aren't you ever going to bed?" Aunt Gwen asked, coming in the room and rummaging around in the closet. She had done something different with her hair, and looked younger than twenty-nine. "Tomorrow's Saturday, you know. There'll be lots to do."

Jean got up and flopped on the cool sheets, annoyed at the nagging. Maybe when you got to twenty-nine, you started turning into your mother. Maybe Aunt Gwen was just getting in some scolding practice before her thirtieth birthday.

Aunt Gwen turned around suddenly with two dresses over her arm. "Good heavens, Jean, why are you staring at me like that?" Her cheeks were pinker now than Jean had ever seen them.

"I didn't know I was staring," Jean said. "I was just noticing your hair. It looks real nice."

The pink in Aunt Gwen's cheeks deepened. "Oh, just some new thing I saw in a magazine." She had her back to Jean now and was sorting through a box on the shelf. "You go on to sleep now. I've some work to do in this closet, but I'll turn out the big light."

Jean turned over and let her arms dangle limply over the sides of the bed. Her eyelids drooped. She could hear Aunt Gwen tiptoeing back and forth between the closet and the dresser. Finally the noise gave way to the night sounds from outside, the moonlight mingled with the glow of the light in the closet, and Jean sank into sleep.

She did not know what time it was when she awoke. Something seemed to have brushed by her arm, bumping the bed. When she opened her eyes, she heard the soft sound of the door closing. She lay perfectly still and listened. There were light footsteps in the hall, a faint creaking of the stairs, and then silence.

She sat up and looked about the room. Aunt Gwen's bed was empty.

There were light footsteps on the gravel of the driveway. Jean threw off the sheet and groped her way to the window in the white nightgown.

Below stood Donald Harvie's clean blue car, the glow of the moon reflecting in its polished top. And there was Donald himself in his Sunday suit, beside Aunt Gwen. Swiftly he picked up the suitcase Aunt Gwen was carrying and placed it on the back seat.

As he closed the car door, however, Aunt Gwen looked nervously up at the house. Suddenly she seemed to freeze, one hand to her throat, and Jean realized that she and Aunt Gwen were staring at each other there in the moonlight.

Donald Harvie looked up too.

"Aunt Gwen!" Jean whispered, kneeling down by the window. "Where are you going?"

In answer, however, Aunt Gwen put one finger to her lips and held it there without moving. Then, she blew a kiss and quickly climbed in the car beside Donald.

Donald Harvie did not start the motor. Instead he released the brake and let the car roll silently down the drive. Only when it had reached the road did the lights come on and the motor start. A few moments later they were gone. Aunt Gwen was gone!

Jean sat motionless, her heart thumping. What was it all about? What should she do?

At first she felt she would run into the next bedroom and tell Mother, but she remembered the pleading way Aunt Gwen had held her finger to her lips. No, Aunt Gwen did not want anybody to know. It was a secret between her and Donald Harvie and Jean.

She crept back in bed and lay staring at the pattern of light and shadow on the walls. She hoped that Gwen and Donald would get a long way off before Grandmother McGinnis found out.

She was almost afraid to get up the next morning, afraid she would give the secret away. She felt she must get out of the room, however, before they came looking for Aunt Gwen. So as soon as she heard the rattle of dishes in the kitchen, she dressed and went downstairs.

Grandmother had on a fresh dress, but her hair still hung in one long braid down her back. As she stirred the oatmeal, she looked out toward the barn.

"I wonder wha's got into the cows?" she said quizzically to Angus. "Just listen to the lowin'. Wonder if Gwen didn't git to them yit."

"Let the girl sleep," said Father. "I'll milk 'em myself." He jokingly flipped his big napkin at Jean's legs as she sat down at the table.

"Is Gwendolyn up yit?" Grandmother asked, putting Jean's oatmeal before her.

"W . . . What?" Jean stammered, hearing perfectly well.

"Where's your aunt?" asked Grandmother. "Is she still abed?"

"No," said Jean. "Her bed's made up."

Grandmother frowned. "Then wha's she dawdlin' at? Must be oot passin' the time o' day wi' Donald Harvie." She grunted and shook her head.

Jean breathed easier now. She'd been asked and had answered. There was no reason they should ask her any more.

By eight o'clock, when Gwendolyn still hadn't appeared, Grandmother went out to the barn to look for herself. Angus was finishing the last of the milking, and Jean sat on a stool beside him to keep out of Grandmother's way.

"Still haven't found her?" Angus asked. "That's funny now."

Grandmother stood for a moment with hands on her hips, thinking. "Well, maybe she made her egg rounds first thing this mornin', though I can't think why she'd go so early. Jean, ye run over to Donald Harvie's an' ask of her there.''

Jean started at a run. She knew very well that Donald wouldn't be there, but she could talk to Tommy Pepper. The door, however, was locked and no one answered her knock.

When she got back, she took a deep breath and went straight to Grandmother. "Nobody's home at Donald Harvie's," she told her.

Grandmother nodded and picked up a pile of fresh sheets for the beds upstairs. "He an' the boy ha'e gone to toon, prob'ly. Donald Harvie always was one for lettin' his shoppin' go till Saturday mornin' 'stead o' doin' it proper Friday nights." She went up the stairs to Aunt Gwen's bedroom. Jean sat down to wait on the sun porch and buried her nose in a magazine.

Almost instantly Grandmother was back down again, her face as white as the eggs on the table. As Angus came in the back door, she looked at him blankly, her lips moving but saying nothing.

"What is it, Mother?" he asked.

"Her clothes are gone, Angus," Grandmother said, so softly it was merely a whisper. "Gwen's run off."

"Run off? Where to? Her car's still here."

Mother got up from the dining room table where she had been cutting out a pattern. "Mom McGinnis, I'm going to drive to the shopping center and ask

141

around," she said. "Surely somebody must have seen her."

She went outside quickly and started Father's car. Angus took a big breath, thrusting his hands in his pockets. "Don't know what good it'll do," he said finally. "If she's gone, she'll not come back till she's ready. Reckon I better take her car and do the egg rounds. Folks'll be callin' if they don't have 'em. Come on, Brian, you can go with me."

Jean sat miserably on the sun porch. How much longer should she keep the secret? Was it fair to have Mother and Father and Grandmother looking all around Oshkosh and worrying themselves sick?

The house was empty except for her and Grandmother. The old lady hobbled back and forth through the rooms, her mouth drawn, and Jean grew more uncomfortable by the minute. Then she had an idea. Maybe Tommy Pepper could tell them something.

"Grandmother," she said. "I could run over to the carnival. I'll bet Tommy's there. He might know."

"I'll not be lettin' ye go alone," said Grandmother. "I'll go too. The walk won't hurt me if we keep to the shade." She picked up the little blue hat she kept on the kitchen shelf and placed it on her head sideways, stuck a handkerchief in her bosom, and they were off down the driveway.

Jean walked slowly so her grandmother could

keep up. Every so often they stopped in the shade, and Grandmother took out her handkerchief to wipe her face.

" 'Tis a sad day, it is, Jean, when one o' your own flesh n' blood runs away an' you've got to carry it aroond in your heart. We didna' get on too well the last month or two, Gwendolyn an' I, an' I can't forget it. I'm sure 'twas tha'."

"You can't be sure, Grandmother," Jean said. "We don't even know where she's gone."

"Aye, but I'm thinkin' and thinkin' on it. 'Tis the first time Gwendolyn an' I've had words, an' the first time she's run off."

They reached the carnival grounds and went over to the donkey tent where Tommy Pepper worked. He was cleaning out the stable.

"How ya doin'?" Tommy propped his shovel against the wall. With an uncontrollable grin, he turned to Grandmother. "Seen any kelpies lately?"

"Listen, Tommy," said Jean, "Do you have any idea where Aunt Gwen might be? We can't find her."

"No kiddin'?" said Tommy. "Just disappeared, huh? Right into thin air!"

Grandmother gasped and sat down on a folding chair outside the tent.

Jean frowned. "No, she just didn't disappear. She's gone with her clothes, and we thought you might know something about it." She studied him carefully.

143

"Haven't seen her since day before yesterday," Tommy said, avoiding the question. "She looked all right to me then. I mean, if she was half-ate by a kelpie, I woulda' noticed."

Grandmother moaned again and Jean glared at Tommy. "Now look, Tommy Pepper, do you know where she is or not?"

"Of course not!" said Tommy. "She could be in Texas for all I know!"

There was something about the way he said it that made Jean suspicious. He must know. How could Donald Harvie go off and leave Tommy alone in the house without telling him?

Grandmother spotted Murray Price across the lot and hurried away. Jean turned to Tommy.

"Listen, Tommy, you'd better tell the truth. When did you last see Donald Harvie?"

Tommy appeared to be thinking, obviously enjoying the game. "Guess it was yesterday afternoon, 'bout four o'clock. He brung me over here with a couple clean shirts and turned me over to Murray."

"He did? Aren't you ever going to see him again?"

"Oh, sure. Week or so, maybe. Reckon I'll see him afore the carnival packs up."

"Why not before a week?" Jean asked, more suspicious than ever. "Surely you'll see him before then."

Tommy Pepper swung himself up on a donkey's back and nudged him out toward the field. "Wouldn't count on it," he called, grinning.

Jean turned and went back to Grandmother who had Murray Price cornered by the concession stand.

"Murray Price, all these years ye've been buyin' milk an' butter from me, wha' d'ye mean makin' a remark like tha'?"

"My dear woman," said Murray, his chin wobbling up and down as he spoke. "I merely voiced my admiration for your splendid daughter! When a girl her age runs away from home, it takes courage! It takes spunk and gumption!"

Grandmother spluttered and blinked her eyes. "A girl her age ha' no business runnin' away from home, Murray Price, an' wha's more, she hasn't a reason!"

"Why, Grandmother McGinnis, what more reason does a woman need than that she's reached the sober age of twenty-nine! My only regret is that she disappeared so suddenly, for I was about to run off with her myself."

"Why, you scoundrel!" cried Grandmother. "You weasel-eyed scoundrel!"

"Now, now, Grandmother," said Murray, nodding toward Jean. "Remember the little folks."

But Grandmother misunderstood. "Ah, Murray, then ye believe in 'em too! I tell ye it's the Little Folk who are behind this, an' 'tis a' because o' tha' Pepper boy. The first day I laid eyes on the lad, I said, 'Tha' boy has an elf on his back sure as my name's

McGinnis!' An' sure enough, if someone didn't let him in our very door, an' to this day there's been nothin' but trouble. The Little People ha'e moved in, lock, stock, an' barrel, an' there's naught we can do except travel over water at night wi' them on our backs, which isn't easy."

Murray Price was enjoying himself hugely. "It's a hot summer ahead," he said in his deep voice, "and the Little Folk have need of a cool cellar. Treat 'em well, Mrs. McGinnis, and maybe you'll get your Gwen back before the autumn sets in."

Jean stared at Murray, aghast. How could he talk such nonsense to Grandmother!

But Grandmother was hurrying off across the field toward home, her eyes on the trees and her ears to the wind. Murray Price sat down on a box, held his big stomach, and shook with silent laughter.

Chapter **11**

WHEN JEAN got back to the house with Grandmother, Angus and Brian were just coming in from making egg rounds.

"No word of 'er," Jean's father said. "Don't see there's much more we can do except wait to hear."

Grandmother McGinnis slowly eased herself into the chair by the lilac bush without a word.

"Well," said Brian, sprawling on the ground beside her. "Maybe Auntie Gwen just got tired of the farm."

"Be quiet, Brian," said Father. "That's hardly the way to speak now."

"Why not?" Brian wanted to know. "I get tired of it. Don't you, ever?"

Big Angus did not answer, but Grandmother did. "Aye, lad," she said, her voice flat and colorless. "Everybody gets tired of the farm now and then, even your granny."

Jean sat quietly on the back steps. Somehow she had thought that Grandmother was as much a part of the farm as the sheep and the barn. Maybe the old lady herself had grown tired of the endless cycle of seasons, on and on, forever and ever.

Mother came up the drive in the car and stopped.

"No news, Rita?" asked Grandmother.

"No. I even asked at the bus depot. No one saw her."

The sun rose higher overhead and the air grew hot. Finally Mother said, "I'm going in and get us some lunch, Mom McGinnis. Why don't you just sit here and let me bring you something?"

The old lady did not answer. Mother went inside and washed her hands at the pump. Jean followed her into the kitchen and watched uncomfortably as she took out the bread and bologna and cut it into thick sandwiches. Suddenly Jean felt she could hold back no longer and said haltingly, "Mother, I've got something to tell you."

"What?" Mother went on cutting the meat, her thoughts far away. But when she got no answer, she looked up. "What is it?"

Jean gulped. "I know about Aunt Gwen. I didn't think I should tell because it was a secret."

"You know?" said Mother. "Know what?"

"I saw her last night from the window. She had her suitcase, and drove away with Donald Harvie."

Mother stared at Jean, her lips parted, her eyes

unbelieving. "She drove away with Donald Harvie? With her suitcase?" Suddenly her face broke into a wide smile and she bent over, hugging Jean hard. "Oh, I'm so glad for her!" she breathed softly. "So glad! So glad!"

Mother wheeled around and started outside toward Grandmother, Jean at her heels, but someone had gotten there first. Brother Bean was sitting in the grass.

"Good morning, Jean!" he called. "Come on over. I want you to hear the good news too." And before anyone could say a word, he added, "I've come with news about your daughter, Grandmother McGinnis. She's now Mrs. Donald Harvie, and she's off on her honeymoon. She asked me to come over this morning and tell you."

Slowly one wrinkled hand rose from her lap, and Grandmother numbly touched her cheek. "Gwendolyn? Married to Donald Harvie?" The hand fell limply in her lap again. "How do you know, Brother Bean?"

"I married them myself, late last night, right there in my tent with the stars looking on. And a happier couple you never saw. I hope you'll give her your blessing when she comes back, Grandmother."

Big Angus gave a whistle. "That's a relief! We've looked the farm over. Couldn't imagine what happened."

"I should have come earlier," the lanky preacher

149

apologized. "Fact is, I slept late."

"Oh, Mom McGinnis, aren't you glad she's all right?" said Mother, stooping over the old woman. "Why, we've all known how she and Donald felt about each other, and it's time they were getting married."

"Mrs. Donald Harvie," Grandmother said, her hand lifting and dropping again in her lap. "My Gwendolyn, up and married in the middle o' the night, an' not a word to her mither."

"Please don't take it hard," said Brother Bean. "She thought it might be easier for you if she did it that way."

"I was just fixing lunch," Jean's mother told the preacher. "Won't you have a bite with us?"

"I'd appreciate it," said the man. "It's cool out here under the trees."

Jean went inside with her mother to finish the sandwiches, and Mother hugged her again. "Oh, I'm so glad for Gwendolyn," she said.

No one was quite sure how Grandmother felt about it. She went silently about her work, pausing every so often to stare distractedly out the window. She did not smile, she did not scold, and no one dared disturb her.

They were hard days for Angus, too. With Aunt Gwen bringing home a husband, it was more urgent than ever to find a house for his family. Like a big,

fair-haired bear he paced the floor, thoughtful, restless and moody.

It wasn't just a house they were looking for, but a
whole farm. They needed at least land enough for
Father to start his herd of dairy cattle and Mother to
have a vegetable garden, and all of them to have a
place of their own.

Every afternoon they climbed in Father's car and
went to look at property. But even the smallest farms
were more than Father could pay.

"It's no use, Angus," Mother said one evening.
"The only thing to do is rent. At least we can use the
land."

Big Angus shook his head. "I won't rent, Rita,"
he said determinedly. "I want to know the land is
mine. I want that feelin'."

The discussion continued well into dinner, with
Grandmother listening disapprovingly from her end
of the table, and Brian interrupting from time to time
to ask for more milk or another spoon or a second
helping of pudding. The tension was mounting,
particularly when Grandmother said at last:

"Maybe it wasn't meant for ye to be a dairy farmer,
Angus. Your faither was satisfied wi' a handful o'
cows wi'oot wantin' twenty or more, an' he found his
peace in tillin' the fields."

"I'm my own man, Mother," Angus replied
sharply. "I got my own mind, and my mind says I

want to have me a dairy farm. I won't rest till I got it."

Grandmother lifted her tea cup and looked across at her son. "Ye want too much, Angus. Ye want the moon an' the stars, an' ye've a pocket full o' sand to buy them wi'."

"Daddy," Jean said timidly, wanting to escape. "I don't want any more supper. Could I go over to Brother Bean's?"

"I don't care where you go," her father snapped irritably. "Can't we have any talkin' without you and Brian interferin'?"

Hurt, Jean rose quickly and went outside. She ran across the yard, her eyes misty. Why take it out on her? It wasn't her fault they were living with Grandmother and needing to get out on their own.

She groped her way through the dark barn, listening to the soft crunching sound of the cows as they ate their hay, and the occasional stomp of a hoof. Lifting the latch on the back door, she went out into the barnyard, closed the gate behind her, and headed out across the cow pasture to the fence beyond. So what if Father did want the moon, and the stars too? Aunt Gwen had a way of turning sand into stardust. Why couldn't he?

Brother Bean, dressed in a new suit as white as lamb's wool, was dusting the folding chairs in his tent and picking up chewing gum wrappers.

152

"Hello, Jean." He smiled and moved to the next row.

Jean sat down and watched him work. And then, because he seemed lost in his own thoughts, she gained the courage to ask, "Brother Bean, did you ever want something you couldn't have? Not a baby pig or clothes or things like that, but something really big, like a whole farm?"

The preacher's hand moved more slowly on the backs of the chairs and he did not look up. "Yes," he said quietly. "A lot of things."

"Like what?"

"Like a car. I've only had that truck, bad as it is, for a year. Before that, all I had were the soles on my shoes."

"What did you do about wanting a car so much?" Jean asked.

Brother Bean stopped dusting. For a moment he stood very still, his bony shoulders motionless beneath the coat of his new white suit.

"I stole one, Jean. Like a common thief, I stole one."

Jean stared. "You just drove away with somebody's car?"

The tall man moved on down the row. "It wasn't that simple. Sin never is. The car belonged to a neighbor of mine who had gone to Tennessee to work for the summer. He left his car behind, and his wife didn't drive, so I decided to borrow it for my revival tour and bring it back in the fall."

"And did you?"

"The police brought it back," said Brother Bean. "And I went to jail for two months. I had it coming, I know. But I still believe I deserved that car more than the wife did."

"But it wasn't yours!" said Jean. "You knew it was wrong."

"Yes, I guess I did. Seems like everything I need is always somebody else's." He turned suddenly, and his face had an intensity that Jean had never noticed before. "I could do so much," he said, "so much, if I weren't worrying all the time about what to eat and what to put on and where the money for repairs is coming from. I've got a lot to give, and a lot to say, but sometimes it's all taken up with worry."

It was a strange confession from the man in the white suit. And yet, in the next breath he was saying, "I know how you want to live on a farm of your own, Jean. I know what it's like with the grandmother. But the world is what we make it. Your house can be a palace or a prison, depends on how your mind sees it. The problem is not how to get what you don't have, but how to make do with what you have while you've got it."

There was the sound of a car in the field outside, and then another. Jean remained motionless in her seat, listening to the hymn that began on the scratchy record player. Brother Bean's soft voice in the back of the tent, welcomed the people inside.

When she finally turned around, she found a tent full of people. Black-hatted ladies and clean-shaven men sat formally in taffeta dresses and pinstriped suits, and she realized in a sudden panic that here she was in the front row with her old cotton denim and her bare feet.

At that moment Brother Bean came down the aisle. When he reached the front, he held up his hand and smiled. "Hymn number 281, Brothers and Sisters, and welcome to the Bean Revival. Let's all sing as though singing would save the world, and maybe it will, maybe it will."

Brother Bean knew the words by heart. Still smiling, he lifted his eyes, took a deep breath, and let his marvelous voice ring out the song. It picked up the weary voices of the tired men and women there in the folding chairs and soared with them over the tops of the trees and out beyond the stars:

Heavenly sunlight, heavenly sunlight,
Flooding my soul with glory divine,
Hallelujah! I'm rejoicing,
Singing His praises, Jesus is mine.

Gone were the old denim dress and the bare feet, gone was the worry over Grandmother and Aunt Gwen and whether or not Father would find a farm. As Jean watched the wonderful man in the snow white suit, singing his heart out, his arms stretched wide, his eyes closed and a forever smile on his face, she felt she had met the most wonderful man on earth. Here was a man who could see beyond the moment, into the beautiful possibilities ahead, and could, if you'd let him, teach you to live forever at peace with yourself.

She was hardly aware of when the singing had stopped and the preaching began. Brother Bean was talking about sin and selfishness, of betting and race tracks and whiskey and carnivals, of fast horses and easy money and liquor and Murray Price. And the more he talked about Murray, the more intently the people listened; the more he talked about the sin-sick ladies and the pitiful freaks and life on the road and in the carnival tents, the more the people said "Amen." And then the music was playing again and Brother Bean was asking people to come to the altar, to come down that sawdust aisle and exchange the sin in their hearts for the glories of eternal life, of health and happiness forever and ever.

As the people came, and the row along the altar grew longer, Brother Bean looked over at Jean and smiled. She did not hesitate. In bare feet and denim dress, she knelt there beside the others, and when Brother Bean came over and put his hand on her head and told her she might live forever, Jean's lips trembled with joy and guilt, relief and confusion. She could not even look into his wonderful face because of the tears that ran down her cheeks and onto the denim.

156

She was conscious suddenly of two strong arms on hers. As she was lifted to her feet, she looked around. There, behind her, was Father, his face gentle but unsmiling. Without a word, he put one arm around her shoulder and ushered her back down the aisle and out into the darkness of the clear summer night.

"Daddy!" Jean said. "It wasn't over."

"It was for you, Jean girl," he said. "You'll not be goin' there again."

"Why?"

"Things are sometimes best left unsaid," he answered, starting with her across the field. "I know you liked the man, and it's well you think of him with likin'. Before, I wouldn't have cared. But it's over now."

He would say no more, and Jean couldn't. Before what? What could Father possibly know about Brother Bean that she didn't? The experience of the evening filled her with strange feelings, and she was almost glad her father had come, but didn't know why.

The following day, Jean was allowed to go to the carnival grounds alone to say good-bye to Tommy Pepper. The carnival was packing up and going east. It would make its long tour through Michigan and Illinois, Indiana and Ohio, on through the south, starting its northward course again and arriving in Oshkosh, as usual, as school let out next year.

Jean put on the yellow dress which Grandmother

157

had made for her, with the matching scarf around her hair. She hadn't said much to Tommy Pepper since the night he rolled cherries off the revival tent, and she was anxious, now, to part friends. She couldn't bear to imagine what the farm would be like without him.

The ferris wheel was already down, and the Zoom was lying on the ground in sections. Tommy was standing with his hands in his pockets, watching the men dismantle the main tent. When he saw Jean, he came over with a shy smile.

"I guess you're leaving this afternoon," Jean said.

"Yeah. Headin' out east, then back through old Kentuck. That's what my Pa liked best, all them hills."

They stood side by side, watching the tent come down, watching the huge mast in the middle telescope into a shorter pole and then big folds of canvas fall in place around it.

"It's going to seem different at school next year without you there," Jean ventured honestly.

"Aw, I'll be around next summer raisin' Cain," said Tommy, thrusting his hands deeper in his pockets.

"Well, I'll miss you anyway," Jean said. "All those stuffy kids."

"They ain't so bad onct you git to know 'em."

They stood there watching the tent go into a van and listening to Murray yelling out instructions through a bullhorn.

"Aunt Gwen is coming home tomorrow," Jean said. "We got a card from them yesterday."

At that moment, Murray Price came across the field holding the leash of a large dog.

"Whose dog is that?" Jean asked.

Murray laughed. "Don't tell me you don't know a Duck-billed, Donkey-tailed, Bird-Dog when you see one!"

Jean stared. "Is *that* it?"

"Minus the bill and tail and wings, it is. But don't you go 'round tellin' my little secret, now."

Jean looked at Murray's enormous face and his small eyes and the big cigar between his teeth, without speaking. There wasn't one thing in the carnival that was pure and true and honest.

"Don't look so shocked, girlie," he said, starting on across the field. "We're all of a kind. There's fraud in us all, even you, and don't forget it."

"I guess I'm just in the way here," Jean said uneasily when he was gone. "I guess you've got to get packed and everything."

"Yeah," said Tommy. "My black tuxedo and twenty pairs of shoes."

They laughed a little.

"Well, have a good time with the carnival," said Jean. "Aunt Gwen'll be sorry she missed you."

Tommy didn't answer, and with another good-bye, Jean turned and headed back to the road.

She felt like crying because nothing was going right. Tommy shouldn't be going off with Murray Price at all. He should be in a house and going to school. She thought again of Brother Bean, that wonderful man with the smiling face and the out-stretched arms, standing there in his white suit and singing his heart out. Murray Price lived in a world that was shady, dishonest, and cheap. But Brother Bean stood for trust and honor, and Jean wished suddenly that Aunt Gwen had married the marvelous man in the white suit instead of Donald Harvie.

She had just crossed the road when she heard the beep of a car behind her. It was Shirley's mother.

"Come and get in, Jean," she called. "It's too hot to walk. Hasn't this been a summer?"

Jean got in. "I was just saying good-bye to Tommy Pepper," she explained. "The carnival's leaving today."

"And it's a good thing, too," Mrs. Aimes said as the car moved forward. "What a disgrace to our village! And the deal with the preacher takes the cake!"

Jean turned. "Brother Bean? What kind of a deal?"

"I just heard it this morning," said Shirley's mother. "Why, that Murray could talk the leaves off the trees. He and the preacher are going to travel together. They'll go into a town, set up the carnival at one end and the revival at the other, and the more the preacher talks against the carnival, the more the people come to listen. And the more they hear, the more they want to see the sideshows he talks about. A real setup, I say."

Jean listened, her face blank. It couldn't be! Brother Bean would never do such a thing!

"So there's profit in it for both," Mrs. Aimes went on. "Somebody said this was the first time Brother Bean had enough money to buy himself a suit. Why, he had a full tent every night after he started preaching about the carnival!" She shook her head. "Folks'll fall for anything. Preach a little sin and they all want to go see."

The car had scarcely stopped at the foot of the drive before Jean got out.

"Thank you, Mrs. Aimes," she said quickly, her face white.

"Jean, dear, you're not sick, are you?" the woman asked, looking at her intently.

"No, I'm all right."

The car rolled on. Jean did not go up the drive. She ran across the vegetable garden, leaping over the rows of beans and tomatoes, flying over the gate to the cow pasture and heading out toward the field beyond. It couldn't be true. There must be another explanation. Brother Bean would never agree to team up with a man like Murray.

She reached the fence by the plum trees and stopped, her chest heaving and her mouth dry. The revival tent, the truck, the chairs, and the big white sign with the black letters were all gone. Even the rails had been put back in the fence. Brother Bean was gone, and all that was left were the two tire tracks in the clover, which led out to the road and disappeared.

Jean lay listlessly on the sun porch, staring up at the streams of light which poured through the wide windows, illuminating the dust particles floating silently about in all directions.

She felt as though she too were floating, that there was neither a piece of ground under her feet nor one sure thing or person she could really count on.

People stopped at nothing to get the things they wanted. She remembered what she had done to Shirley Aimes. If Brother Bean could team up with Murray, what might Tommy Pepper do to get a pig? What might Father do to get a farm? How did you really learn to "make-do," to turn sand into stardust, to make a wee moon? Only Aunt Gwen seemed to know the secret, but she had run off and married a crude, coarse farmhand, and Jean doubted that her moon was worth having at all.

She felt somewhat better that afternoon. The house was tidied up for Aunt Gwen's arrival, and the kitchen smelled of homebaked rolls and custard pie. When at last the crunch of tires sounded on the gravel driveway, Jean flung herself out the door and into Aunt Gwen's arms.

"Jean! Oh, it's good to be back!" Aunt Gwen held her at arm's length. "Honestly, Jean, you look like a young lady. You really do."

Jean was conscious of the tall man behind Gwen, his neck brown and wrinkled from the sun. He was smiling, and Jean wondered if she'd ever seen him smile before. She felt she had to say something, so she said, "Hello, Uncle Donald."

The tall man stared back without answering. Then he glanced at Gwen and they both started laughing.

"Why, that does sound funny, doesn't it?" laughed Gwen.

Donald Harvie grinned. "You can call me anythin' you like, Jean. Donald will do."

Grandmother was embarrassed when they came in the kitchen. She gave them a quick smile and continued to bustle about the stove, tending to pots which didn't have to be looked after.

"Didn't think ye'd git here till six or after, way traffic is on the roads," she burbled, opening the oven and closing it again.

"Mother." Gwen's eyes twinkled. "Don't I even get a hug?"

Grandmother's lips trembled. She laid her spoon on the stove and, with her head turned to one side, hurried across the room and threw her arms around Gwen, hugging the tall woman to her and sniffing back the tears.

"There, there," comforted Gwen. "I'm back and we're all together, and I'm so happy I can't bear to see anyone cry."

Grandmother sniffed again, dabbed at her eyes, and timidly put out her hand to Donald Harvie.

Donald smiled down at her. "I'll be good to her, Ma McGinnis," he said. "Don't you worry."

"I know ye will," said Grandmother. "I know ye will."

Dinner that evening was a festive occasion, with fresh flowers on the table. Aunt Gwen talked so much she scarcely ate. She told about the places they'd been and the things they'd seen. She looked like a bird, Jean decided, which had been shut up in a cage all its life and suddenly allowed to fly. Even her hands fluttered as she talked, as though she herself had discovered the world beyond Oshkosh.

"Marriage agrees with you, Gwen," big Angus said, looking at his sister. "I think you made a good choice. And a Scotsman to boot!"

"I do too," said Mother. "It's nice to have you a part of the family, Donald."

For a moment there was silence. Then Grandmother spoke. "Gwen," she said, her eyes on her plate. "I'll not be needin' the big house mysel' wi' Angus and Rita movin'. I didn't ha'e a chance to buy ye a weddin' present before ye married, but I'd lik' to gi' ye this house, hopin' ye'll let me stay."

"If I'll let you!" Gwendolyn said. "Why, of course

you'll stay! What kind of a house would it be without you? The kelpies and the Wee Folk would go where you went, and the place would never be the same. I love this house, Mother, and we were hoping you'd ask us to live here."

Grandmother looked at her new son-in-law. "Nobody knows the land like ye do, Donald, an' the cows are used to ye too. 'Tis only right tha' ye should be the man o' the place wi' Angus movin' away."

"Have you found a farm, Angus?" asked Gwen.

"Not yet," said Angus, "but we're lookin'."

As the pie was passed around, Aunt Gwen said suddenly, "Where's Tommy?"

"He's gone with the carnival," Father told her. "I saw the vans pull out yesterday. Didn't you know?"

Gwen turned to Donald and their eyes showed their alarm.

"Gone?" Gwendolyn exclaimed. "We didn't think they'd go for another week yet! We thought we had plenty of time!"

"They went early," said Angus. "Murray made a sort of deal with the traveling preacher, and word got around. Guess they figured it was best to get out."

Donald leaned forward. "But the boy. I suppose he thought he had to go."

"Why?" asked Mother. "What's wrong?"

"We wanted Tommy to live with us," Aunt Gwen explained. "We told him we were getting married and hoped to adopt him, but he wasn't sure he wanted that. The plan was that he would stay with Murray till we got back, and that would give him a chance to make up his mind. I guess he made it up."

"He told me he was leaving," Jean said. "He didn't say anything about living with you."

"Maybe if we'd been here it would have been different," said Donald, staring moodily across at Gwen. "I'd gotten so fond of the lad, it'll be hard gettin' by without him."

Jean pushed her plate away and hoped no one noticed. Why couldn't Aunt Gwen have come home just one day sooner? Why did things always have to work out wrong? Always.

Chapter *12*

THE LITTLE FOLK were moving in. Grandmother was sure of it. No sooner had Gwen and her husband gone down to the cottage by the river than things began to happen.

It was a black night, with only a sliver of moon. Jean had just crawled into bed when she heard a faint sound, like somebody calling her name. She sat up and listened.

Someone downstairs had heard it too, for there were footsteps in the kitchen and the snap of the lightswitch on the back porch. Hurriedly, Jean got out of bed and went down. Grandmother was there, her long braid hanging down her back, her eyes large and gray.

"Di' ye hear it too, lass?" she asked. "Someone callin' your name?"

"Yes," said Jean. "But far away, like a whisper."

The old lady sat down on a chair, one hand to her throat. "Jean, Jean, do not step oot o' the house wi'oot your faither wi' ye. 'Tis the fairy queen or a kelpie as sure as I've Scotch in my blood." Suddenly she leaped off the chair, her eyes like two fried eggs, and began backing away from the table. "Jean! Look there! Look, lass, look!"

"What, Grandmother?"

"The pie. The second pie we didna' touch."

There in the center of the table sat the second pie, right where Grandmother had left it. And there, near the edge, was a hole about the size of a nickel, as though some wee person had helped himself to a thimbleful of custard.

" 'Tis my fault," moaned Grandmother. "Always before when I'm bakin', I leave a mite for the Wee Folk, but this time, I'd my mind on Gwen."

"It might have been Brian," Jean ventured.

"The lad was abed before I ever put it oot," Grandmother declared. "Quick, lass, to bed!" She bolted the door leading to the porch. "I knew it 'ud happen. When the Pepper lad left, the elf on his back stayed behind, an' noo he's movin' into oor house an' will soon be on one o' us wi' a' his tricks. Hurry, Jean, off to bed, an' call i' ye hear the voice again!"

Jean scrunched down under the covers, her wide eyes peeping out. Of course it was ridiculous nonsense. What could she possibly have that a fairy queen,

168

if there were such a thing, could want? No money, no jewels, not even a bracelet from the five and ten. And suddenly she remembered the dollhouse.

Of course! Why wouldn't the Wee Folk want it? Not even fairies could build such a magnificent house as she and Aunt Gwen had made. Why not give it to them? Why not be the only girl in the whole United States who owned a dollhouse inhabited by Scottish fairies? She smiled to herself, wishing it were true. Tomorrow, if Grandmother were still upset, she would suggest it.

It wasn't only Grandmother who was upset the next day. Jean came downstairs to find Brian bellowing loudly. The candy bar which Donald Harvie had given him the night before was gone, and also the cream which Mother had set aside for the porridge. But that wasn't all. Big Angus came up from the shower to report that a basement window was open and half the apples in a basket were missing. Later, when they all sat down to breakfast, Jean found a tiny blue bow on the floor, the tiniest ribbon she had ever seen.

Grandmother needed no more convincing. The Little People were already in, and there would be no end to their tricks. Needles would disappear, plates would crack, flowers would wilt, milk would sour, porridge would burn, and feet would ache. There was no way to get rid of the Wee Folk except to wait till they got on your back and then travel over water at night, which wasn't likely to happen.

It was delightful fun, however, even if they only half believed it. Brian whooped and shouted and caused half the trouble himself, but no matter what he did, Grandmother blamed it on the fairies.

"Grandmother," Jean said that afternoon. "I know why the fairies were calling my name. I think I know what they want."

Grandmother fixed her eyes on Jean, her mouth open.

"The dollhouse," said Jean. "It's just the right size, isn't it? Why, it's perfect for them! Why don't we put it out in the barn, and maybe they will go live in it there."

Grandmother sat down, thinking. "Lass, you've a clear head," she said finally. "Of course 'tis wha' they want. A fairy queen should ha'e such a house!"

They carried it to the barn and set it on two bales of hay. Then Grandmother stocked the little kitchen with raisins, bits of bread, cookie crumbs, apple slices, and peanuts.

"We will not come back till the milkin' tonight," she said, closing the door to the barn, leaving the small house to the Wee Folk.

The rest of the day went as usual. Gwen and Donald came for supper again. As Jean and her aunt were clearing the dishes later, Jean showed her the small blue bow she had found on the floor. "Who else but a fairy would wear such a tiny bow?" she asked.

170

Aunt Gwen picked it up between her thumb and finger, a smile spreading across her face.

"I'll tell you who, Jean," she whispered. "A brand new bride might wear just such a bow on her garter. Something old, something new, something borrowed, something blue." Her eyes twinkled.

"Then it's yours?" Jean asked.

"Yes, but you keep it for good luck," her aunt said, and they laughed together.

It was later than usual when Grandmother went to the barn to milk the cows, and Jean went along. The food in the doll house was gone, every crumb.

Grandmother looked at Jean. "It may ha'e done it, lass. It may ha'e moved 'em oot. You're a smart lass, ye are, an' a credit to the McGinnises."

Jean only smiled and wished she could believe in the Wee Folks herself.

As she sat down on the foot stool by the brown cow, Grandmother started the old familiar song she always sang to her pet:

I've heard the lilting, at our yowe milking,
Lassies a-lilting, before the dawn o' day. . . .
but suddenly she stopped. "Maybe it's the turn o' the moon, but I'll miss him too, tha' boy."

Jean continued stroking the cow's warm brown side. "Tommy Pepper?"

"Aye, an' I do na' know why. But there were times he made me laugh to mysel', an' 'tis good to ha'e somethin' to laugh at noo an' then."

"Maybe when he comes back next year, Aunt Gwen can persuade him to stay," Jean said. She smiled impishly. "Of course, if he still has an elf on his back, it wouldn't do to let him in the house."

Something hit Jean on the arm and she looked down. It was a piece of a mud dauber's nest. A moment later another piece landed at her feet, and then something hit the milk pail with a loud "ping."

Jean looked up to the rafters. There, in the window above the hay loft, sat Tommy Pepper.

"Hi, mole," he said grinning, and as Jean gasped, he swung himself out over the hay and landed on his knees in the light of the lantern. Grandmother's mouth dropped open and her hands hung motionless above the pail.

"Tommy!" Jean cried, as the boy stood up and shook the hay from his clothes. "I thought you were gone!"

"I was," said Tommy. "Got clear to Michigan before a kelpie come along and carried me back."

Grandmother McGinnis slowly dropped her hands in her lap. "Tommy Pepper," she said sternly, "wha' happened wi' ye? I want the truth, noo."

"Thirty miles out of town I changed my mind," Tommy said. "I told Murray I'd rather live on the farm with the kelpies and my new mom and dad, and he give me two bucks for the bus ride back." He laughed and dug in his pocket, pulling out the money.

"But I didn't spend it on the bus. I walked. And now I'm two dollars rich."

Grandmother McGinnis looked at the boy before her, his legs slightly bowed in his faded jeans, and his dirty tee shirt hanging limp over his hips. His dusty hair covered his large blue eyes, and his small bony chin had a determined thrust.

Grandmother stood and picked up the lantern. "Tommy, ha'e ye ate?"

"No'm, not much."

Grandmother waited a moment, smiling faintly. "Are ye hungry?"

"I know I got a stomach," Tommy replied. "It's been talkin' to me all the way back."

Grandmother smiled broadly this time. "Come in the house, lad. Mind you wash at the pump an' I'll set ye a plate."

It was a gay procession. Grandmother went first, eager to break the news to Gwendolyn. But Gwen needed no telling. She looked up from the sink where she was washing dishes and a moment later had her big arms about Tommy. He looked like a colt being petted for the first time, surprised that he liked it, Jean decided.

"Then you've come back," Donald Harvie said, putting his hands on the boy's shoulders. "It was a sad bit of news that you were gone, but we're glad you're back, lad."

Tommy ate as though his stomach had been empty

all year. Grandmother was delighted.

"Aye, there'll be plenty to do wi' this lad around," she said. " 'Tis like Angus when he was little. A lot o' work to keep one stomach full."

"Tommy," Jean whispered, as Grandmother put the butter back in the refrigerator. "How long have you been here? Did you see anyone in the barn today?"

"Just myself," said Tommy. "Pretty good lunch you put out for me, too. Awful small helpin's, though."

Jean's eyes opened wide. "In the dollhouse? Did you . . ."

Tommy only grinned and went on eating as Grandmother came back in the kitchen. But when she went out again for wood, Jean whispered quickly, "Tommy, were you here last night? Were you around without our knowing it?"

"Maybe I was and maybe I wasn't."

"Oh, Tommy!" Jean giggled. "You called my name, didn't you? And you stuck your finger in the pie and took Brian's candy bar and came in the cellar window. I should have known it was you!"

"Just wanted to see how you all got along without me," Tommy said, picking up the pie crust in his hands and taking big bites of it. "And you didn't git on so good, what with fairies runnin' all over the place, eatin' the pie and stealin' apples!"

It was good having Tommy back, even if he did act

like he owned the place. He rode the brown mare all over the farm, patrolling the river, riding herd on the three cows in the evening, and whistling a maddening carnival tune.

Jean was sitting on the rock by the driveway a few days later, watching the mare trotting around the clover field with Tommy on her back. There was a skidding of wheels behind her, and Angus' car came speeding up the drive.

"Aunt Gwen around?" he asked, leaning across the seat.

"I think she went shopping," Jean answered.

Her father opened the door on Jean's side. "Get in, lass," he said, smiling broadly. "I'm goin' loony and got to have someone along."

"What?" Jean said, climbing in the car and noticing the sparkle in his eyes. "Going where?"

"Loony, lass, loony. I found a place to live and your mother hasn't even seen it. She'll be sayin' my mind's gone, that's what."

"A house!" Jean quickly closed the door as the car began backing down the drive. "Is it far?" she asked.

"Close as the right hand is to the left," replied big Angus.

"Is it big?" Jean questioned, delighted with the news.

"Big as a barrel of cider," her father said, grinning.

"Oh, Daddy! Tell me about it. Is it pretty?"

The grin on Big Angus' face disappeared and he

grew solemn. "It's different, Jean," he said. "It's goin' to take some doin', but it's got a good roof to keep us dry."

Good heavens, Jean thought. What is it? A barn? Was Father so desperate he'd buy anything?

At the top of the hill, Father turned and drove down the bumpy dirt lane. And suddenly the car stopped.

"There it is," said Big Angus.

"Where?" asked Jean, bounding out the door. "I don't see any house. All I see is the. . ."

The school! Jean stared at her father and then at the little brick schoolhouse. The playground was overgrown with weeds, almost hiding the "For Sale" sign in front, and the windows were dirty and streaked. Its shingled roof was dwarfed by the tall pines, and the front door swayed loosely on one hinge.

Live in this? Jean thought in dismay. *Live back here on an old dirt road in a house with blackboards on the walls and a big brass bell perched crazily atop the roof? Live in a house with a playground for the front lawn and names of untold students carved in the steps and the door frames?*

Big Angus began talking quickly as he started up the path, Jean behind him. "Wouldn't be anythin' like a dream house, I know. The road's not paved and there's no barn. I'd have to put 'em in myself. But this house would stand for many a year, and the land's good. Property reaches all the way down to the river, with good fields on either side."

Jean squeezed through the half-open door and followed her father up the stairs, down the hall, and into the large classroom, her head spinning with disbelief. Was this what they'd come back for—all the way from West Virginia? Was this the place she'd tell her friends she was going to live?

There was a sense of urgency in her father's voice as he led her to the window and pointed out the big sweep of land, reaching down to the trees along the river. "Good green fields," he said. "Good grazin' for cattle. And the house is well built. Look at the flooring, Jean. You don't see houses built like this anymore. Good solid timber, and good thick walls. It's a sturdy place."

Jean had not said a word since they'd come inside. She wished that Mother was here . . . or Aunt Gwen. Her eyes jumped from window to window in the long row of them along one wall. It was a huge room— the whole second floor, almost. If they put in some walls and made it into bedrooms, every bedroom would have at least two windows. That wasn't bad.

She walked quickly to the door of the classroom and looked at the long wide hall with its rows and rows of coat hooks. ". . . and out here, Daddy," she said, as though she'd been talking to him all the time, "we could build a long closet that reached from one end of the hall to the other and hold all our clothes! And downstairs. . ." She ran down the hall and clattered to the first floor, her father behind her. "See? Down here we'd have the kitchen at one end, and the rest would be living room, where the fireplace is."

"And two bathrooms both sides the stairs with no tubs in either," smiled big Angus.

But the dream had begun in Jean, and there was no stopping her now. To make a wee moon—to turn a schoolhouse into a home—would be no small task, but it would be theirs.

"Oh, Daddy, it's crazy! But it's wonderful! I mean, it will be wonderful some day! All the things we can do with it! I've got so many ideas I'm ready to burst."

Father smiled at her proudly, pleased that she liked it. "You've a busy head, Jean," he said, "A lass who can see beyond the ordinary look of things."

"You too," said Jean. "How did you ever think of it?"

"Well, it's somethin' we can afford," said big Angus. "I heard the men at the feed store say the school board was anxious to sell. They can't find anyone willin' to take the school down and haul it away. So I said to myself, I'll buy the land and leave the schoolhouse right there, and that's where we'll live."

"It's time for Mother to come home," Jean said excitedly. "Let's go pick her up and bring her here. I can't wait to show it to her."

Father went outside and climbed in the car as Jean

scrambled in the other side. "Let's dream no dreams till your mother sees it," he said. "Dream no dreams."

Mother was outnumbered, but she didn't mind. Jean and big Angus chattered like magpies all the way to the school. They rushed her up and down stairs, around the playground, down the hill to the river and back again, scarcely letting her speak, afraid of what she might say. Finally Mother sat down on one of the desks and pulled Jean to her.

"You know," she said, "I think the four of us are going to make this one of the prettiest little houses around Oshkosh."

"I knew you'd like it!" Jean cried delightedly. "I knew you would."

Father came over and put one arm around Mother. "Do you think we've gone loony, lass?" he said. "Did you ever think we'd be buyin' a school?"

"No," smiled Mother. "But I like surprises, and this is one of the best. I can't wait to tell Gwen!"

It was all over the village, maybe all over Oshkosh, for all Jean knew. When she made the egg rounds with her aunt several days later, everyone had heard about it.

"Is it true, Jean, that your father bought the old schoolhouse and your family is actually going to live in it?" people asked curiously.

No, Jean wanted to answer. We're going to use it for a bowling alley.

"Yes," she would say instead, half embarrassed, half proud. "It's true."

She hardly even saw her parents the next few days. There were papers to sign and lawyers to see and banks to visit, and a hundred other details. Aunt Gwen was busy in the little cottage by the river, sorting things for the move to the farmhouse. Grandmother was packing Jean's and Brian's clothes, and Tommy Pepper was hanging around like yesterday's leftovers, feeling strangely out-of-place. He had no room yet of his own, no real place to put his few possessions, and Jean sensed his discomfort.

"Grandmother," she said, coming in the kitchen. "Would you do something very, very special as a going-away present for me?"

"Ye feel the need o' a present for leavin' your granny behind?"

"Oh, Grandmother, that's not it," Jean said, putting her arms around the wide waist and giving her a hug. "It's special for Tommy Pepper."

Grandmother McGinnis gave a grunt. "Aye. What's he wantin' now? A chocolate cake?"

"No. I want you to give him a pig."

Grandmother turned slowly around and raised her shaggy eyebrows. "A pig, lass? A live pig or a cured one?"

"A little live pig. One for his very own, to feed and raise and sell when it's grown, if he wants to."

"If he wants to feed the pigs and raise 'em, I've no

voice ag'in it," said Grandmother.

"But he's got to know that it belongs to him," Jean insisted. "You've got to give it to him specially. Please do it, Grandmother."

At that moment Tommy Pepper came in on the back porch and pumped a dipper of water. Grandmother was not one to make a ceremony.

"Tommy, is it ye?" she asked.

"It's me," said Tommy.

The old woman wiped her hands on her apron and waddled over to the door. "Tommy," she said, " 'Ud ye like a pig?"

Tommy put down the dipper. "A pig! You mean it?"

"To raise and to feed and sell at market or what ha'e ye," said Grandmother, impatient to have it done.

"A pig!" Tommy said again, as though he had not heard. "Sure I want a pig! Sure I do!"

"Then go choose it, lad," Grandmother said, waving her apron at him. "Go choose ye one and make it yours an' we'll see how ye do."

She went back to the sink, her eyes smiling, but Tommy continued to stare, his mouth open.

"Did you hear what she said, Jean? She gave me a pig!"

"Did she, now?" asked Jean, laughing. "She's apt to change her mind, you know."

With a whoop and a handspring, Tommy Pepper was off over the yard to the barn, and Grandmother watched him fondly out the window.

"Some folks want gold, an' some want silver, an' some find their peace in a pig," she said to no one in particular. "I'm gittin' to like the boy. I really am."

Jean was picking beans in the garden out near the road when Donald Harvie drove in with the mail.

"Postcard for you, Jean," he called.

Jean wiped one arm across her forehead. "Who's it from?" she asked, coming over.

Donald grinned. "Not my business, now, is it?" He handed her the card. "I'm takin' the boys to the river for a swim. If you've a mind to, why don't you come along?"

Jean's eyes scanned the card. "Maybe," she said, turning away, and her new uncle drove on.

It was a picture postcard of an apple orchard from somewhere in Michigan. It said on the back:

Dear Jean,

By now you know I am gone, and the horses have the clover to themselves again. People like to talk, and I'm sure you've heard plenty. I hope you won't hold it against me. I've always known I wouldn't live forever, but I'd like to see you try it.

Your good friend,
Brother Bean.

Jean stared at the card a long time, turning it over in her hand. It did not upset her as much as she

182

thought it might. Did she miss him, she wondered? No, she missed the man she'd thought he was, not the man in the new white suit who had teamed up with Murray. But she wasn't sure. Maybe it was possible to like a person partly, and partly not like him at all.

She stuck the card in her pocket and walked up to the house, somewhat moody. Tommy Pepper came out in his swimming trunks, Brian at his heels.

"Going swimming, mole?" Tommy said.

"I don't feel like it."

"Come on and watch us, then."

Jean tagged along and lay on the bank while the boys splashed about in the water. Donald Harvie swam awhile too, then crawled out, shaking himself like a dog.

Jean shielded her eyes from the sun, watching the water drop off his elbows and the lobes of his great ears.

"Better change your mind, Jean," he said. "River's coolest thing around here." He sat down on the bank, chewing a weed and looking out over the water.

"Will you be sorry to be moving?" Jean asked suddenly, surprised that she felt like talking to anybody, especially him.

"Yep. Folks always hate a change, even when it's good for 'em. That little shack's been home for a year now, and it's hard to let it go. But there's room in the big house for my books, and it's a library there well as here. Long as I can have my books, I get by. I can travel to South America, build the first railroad, fight the Dakota winters, or cross the desert. With books like mine, lass, I can do anything in the world that pleases me, and the feelin's good. Doesn't matter where the books are stacked, long as they're there when I want 'em."

Why, he talks like Aunt Gwen! Jean mused. Beneath his cowboy hat, he had a head full of stories just waiting to be told, if anybody cared to ask him. He wasn't what he had seemed, anymore than Brother Bean was, and she felt suddenly that she was meeting the tall man Gwen had married, for the first time.

"Donald," she said, resting her head in her hand. "What did you think of the preacher?"

"Brother Bean? Can't help likin' him, you know, since it was him that married your aunt and me."

"But what do you think of him now, after what he did?"

"Same as I did before," said Donald. "I'm sorry about that, all right, but he was only a man, same as the rest of us."

"But you wouldn't do it!" Jean protested. "Or Father. You'd never team up with Murray."

"We weren't in his shoes, lass. Brother Bean was slowly starvin'. You could see it in his eyes. Once he paid for his gas from place to place and the rent of a field, he was lucky to have enough left over for soup, they tell me. Starvin' does strange things to a man, and a man's all he was. When Murray bought him some food and a suit and repaired his truck, it gave

184

him a feelin' of what could be. Then it was easy to change things around in his head, to believe what he was doin' wasn't so bad."

"Do you believe what he said about living forever?"

Donald Harvie smiled. "It has a nice sound, lass, but wantin' doesn't make it true. I'm satisfied to do a good job in the time I've got without wantin' a sky full of stars besides."

He was happy sitting there, this man Jean was only getting to know. He loved Aunt Gwen and the out-of-doors and lived a hundred different lives inside the covers of his books.

She felt a sudden happy feeling about Aunt Gwen and Mother and Father, about herself and the old schoolhouse they were buying. In fact, a moment later she stood up and jumped feet first into the river, skirt and all. When she looked up, laughing, the hair stringing down her face, Donald Harvie was actually laughing, too.

"Thought you weren't going to swim in a muddy old river," Tommy yelled.

But Jean didn't hear. She floated lazily about on her back, her hair spread out on the water. She felt as though she were magic. She could not only change a pear box into a dream house and a school into a home, but she could even turn a somber, sun-baked man like Donald Harvie into a friendly, storytelling uncle. And yet it was really she who had changed.

If she took things only as they seemed and did not
bother to look beneath the surface, they stayed as
they were. It was the looking for hidden possibilities
which brought out the magic in the things and people
around her, even Grandmother.

"Look at me, Jean!" Brian called. "Watch me blow
bubbles!" He stuck his head under the water and
came up muddy.

"You look like Tommy's pig," Jean laughed. "You
know, Tommy, you chose the dirtiest one of the litter.
You really did."

"That's what makes 'im so special," Tommy
grinned. "Know what I named 'im, Jean? M.P. That's
'is name."

"M.P.?" said Jean puzzled, and then her face lit up.
"Oh, Tommy, you awful thing! You didn't!"

"Murry's gotta have somethin' named after 'im,"
Tommy grinned. "Ain't nobody goin' to put up no
statue."

Jean and her aunt went to look at the school, soon
to be a house. It could, Jean realized, stay a schoolhouse in her mind. Every time she went upstairs she
could think, "This is where the desks were." Or she
could, instead, see it as a most unusual house with a
thousand possibilities.

"To make a wee moon," said Aunt Gwen, walking
slowly down the hall and looking at the long row of
coat hooks on one side, "all you need are several gallons

of paint and a strong back. But think what you can do!"

They figured that Jean's room would be on the second floor at the back, with two windows side by side, facing the river. They went downstairs and giggled convulsively over the two bathrooms with no bathtubs. They went outside and down the hill to the river, where Father's dairy cows, which were not even born yet, would some day go. There was no barn yet, no fence, no silo, no haystack, nothing but land, dotted with trees and covered by a great uncluttered expanse of sky.

No matter that the road leading in was dirt, or that there were two baths and no bathtub. No matter that there were no walls between rooms or even a closet. It was the start of a house, and they could turn it into whatever they liked.

It was twilight when Jean and her aunt started home. Tommy Pepper was sitting on the big rock by the drive, carving a belt out of an old harness which Donald Harvie had given him.

"Thought the kelpie got ya," he said, looking up.

"Oh, we've been having the most marvelous time, Tommy," said Aunt Gwen. "We've been looking at the old schoolhouse and fixing it up! Why, we've got the walls in, and the curtains are even up in Jean's room!"

Tommy stared open-mouthed. "Already?"

Aunt Gwen laughed and went gaily on up the

drive. "Only in our heads, of course, but that's where it all begins."

There was only one light burning in the kitchen. Mother and Father had gone to Oshkosh to see about a refrigerator. Donald Harvie was in the barn milking, and only Grandmother waited in the kitchen, fuming noiselessly over a pan she was keeping warm in the oven.

" 'Tis a wonder ye've not caught the fever!" she declared as Jean and her aunt walked in. "Oot at night in this change o' weather, wi' the moon full an' Wee Folk a' aboot. Gwendolyn, I declare, ha'e ye no sense?"

"We've been decorating!" Aunt Gwen smiled, sitting down quickly at the table. "Oh, it's going to be a wonderful house they've got, Mother."

Grandmother grunted as she brought the pan from the oven. "Brian's abed an' a' the folks is at their chores. I'd a mind to come after ye."

Aunt Gwen ate hurriedly, leaving her pie till later so she could help her husband with the milking. But Jean dawdled lazily at the table, savoring the blackberry pie in her mouth, and watching Grandmother lumber about the kitchen, stopping now and then with her hands on the counter to peer through the white curtain at the moon and the mist above the garden.

Tommy Pepper came in and sat on top of the woodbox, scraping intently at the belt he was making and stopping to rub the edge across the sole of his shoe to smooth it.

It was a good time to be alive, Jean decided, scraping her fork across the pie plate and licking the tines. It was a good time to be in Oshkosh, to be moving into a house that was supposed to be a school.

"Grandmother," she said, unable to contain her mischief. "There was mist on the clover tonight."

"Aye, an' the Little People are in the pasture," said the old lady. "Stay away from the fields while the moon is full, for i' ye hear the tinkle of bells and see a small light comin' toward ye in the grass an' hear the callin' o' your name, 'tis the elf queen, sure as my name's McGinnis."

Jean and Tommy exchanged glances. Tommy hid his smile in the crook of his arm and went on carving.

"Tell us about her, Grandmother," said Jean, not wanting to get up.

"Aye, tha's a' there's to do, I suppose—tell tales," said Grandmother gruffly. "Ye've heard them a', lass."

"But Tommy hasn't, Grandmother. Really, don't you think he should know, if he's going to be part of the family?"

Grandmother stopped her bustling and slowly dried the stew pan, looking out the window again at the red glow from the lantern in the barn. " 'Tis such a night as this tha' the fairy queen hersel' comes oot, lad, an' 'tis the truth. I've seen her many a time mysel' in Skye. The first time, long, long ago, I peeked through a knothole in the barn, holdin' a four-leaf clover in my hand, an' there she was, dressed in green, sittin' on the hay, an' by the time I'd my glasses on to make sure, she was gone."

Grandmother McGinnis had the look of a troll about her as she stood at the window, her small nose wrinkled up as she spoke. Like Aunt Gwen and her imagination, Grandmother carried around with her a wee bit of Scotland to liven the cold winters, to soften the summer sun, and to comfort her in the restless changing of the seasons.

"There was an old lady from Oshkosh. . . ." Jean said aloud to herself before she'd realized it. Tommy Pepper looked up from across the room, a quizzical expression on his face. But Grandmother McGinnis didn't notice. On and on her quavery voice crooned, telling the stories of long ago—her eyes on the trees and her ears to the wind.